PHTHALO BLUES

WILL WALLNER

·

ISBN: 1542886503
ISBN-13: 978-1542886505

DEDICATION

This book is dedicated to anyone who's ever been bold enough to follow their dreams. To anyone who's ever tried to accomplish something, which others have said couldn't be done. Nothing inspires me more than people who try to achieve greatness.

CONTENTS

THE RETURN OF KRONOS

A myth passed down through generations tells the story of two legendary warriors; Kronos and Toki. As mortal enemies, they waged war through space and time causing death and destruction far across the galaxy. This is the story of their final battle…

In the night sky, out in the wilderness, a lone wolf drinks from a lake. A full moon illuminated the area with a soft glow. The water rippled gently and glistened with starlight reflection. As the wild dog lifted her head, she sensed something was about to happen. Her eyes were full of Phthalo Blue and she looked out far into the distance. A portal to another dimension began to tear a hole in the sky. Red lights started to flicker in the clouds and lightning poured out of the rift. It burned with Alizarin Crimson. A black crow flew through the sky and ascended towards the gateway. The wolf watched from far away, as the crow flew directly into the eye of the storm. In a flash of red energy the crow vanished. A lightning bolt struck the ground beneath, scorching the earth. From the flames, a dark figure appeared. Witnessing this, the wolf ran from the lake towards the edge of a cliff. She howled through the night, and the sound echoed across the valley beneath.

1 MYSTIC MOUNTAIN

Valley Village, Middle Continent
Day 1 Month 1 Year 2037

The sun began to rise early, on this warm summer day. Birds were singing and the sky was clear. The landscape was mostly untouched by man. Large mountains pierced the sky and were surrounded by a thick blanket of beautiful tall lush green trees. The air smelled as fresh as could be. Other than the sounds of the birds, you could hear a gentle stream as it cascaded along a soft muddy bank. This place was far away from large populations. There were, however, small villages scattered around the valleys. The local villagers lived a simple life and lived in harmony with the nature around them.

Amongst the villages, was a small path, which led up to a single wooden cabin. Trees either side of the footpath created a natural tunnel, which led to a small opening. There the cabin stood, surrounded by grass and small flowers. The rear of the cabin was protected by the slope of a mountain with the stream running down the left side. This cabin was built by an artist many years ago. Over the years, the surrounding vegetation had begun to engulf the wooden cabin, and reclaim it back to nature. The artist was a painter who enjoyed a secluded lifestyle. He built the cabin as a retreat where he could paint uninterrupted. The only company he enjoyed was from small creatures, such as squirrels, who he would feed and allow into his private world. The painter lived a long life and died some years ago. The cabin now served as the temporary residence to a young man. Nearby villagers suggested he use the cabin as it had no use since the artist's death.

The man awoke early on this day and began his morning with a cup of freshly brewed coffee. The aromatic beans filled his cabin as he gazed over at several paintings piled up in the corner. These were mostly old paintings left by the artist, but on top of the pile were a few newer paintings. At the very top, was a simple painting which captivated the young man. The left side was filled with soft blue, the right with bright red, and in the middle, the two colors met to create a shade of deep purple. He stepped outside of the cabin and took a deep breath of fresh air then closed his eyes. The air reminded him of another time in his life. A time he couldn't quite remember clearly. He looked out towards the horizon, deep within his thoughts.

A bird perched on a branch caught his eye. The bird also seemed to be contemplating, as it twitched its head looking in different directions. As the man turned around to reenter the cabin and pour himself another cup of coffee, he heard gentle footsteps coming up the path.

"Taz! I was wondering when you'd get here?" The young man said with his back to the small boy.

"Sorry, I had to help my Uncle with the chickens." Taz replied, slightly out of breath.

"Don't worry, I'm kidding. It's a good thing you brought your cloak, it might get cold up there." The young man entered the cabin and sat down at a wooden table. He pulled a chair out for Taz and arranged several objects on the table.

"Hey, Buck what's this knife for?" Taz asked inquisitively.

"Taz, my name is not Buck. That's just the nickname your Uncle gave me after the villagers found me. I'd rather you didn't call me that."

"So what should I call you? Did you finally remember your real name?"

"I still don't remember anything..." The young man sighed.

"Then how about I call you something else. Something cool, like Dragon?" Taz had a sarcastic grin on his face. "So tell me Dragon, what's the knife for?"

"You never know what might happen up that mountain. I'd hate to have to explain to your Uncle that you were eaten by a wild animal or something."

"I thought my Uncle told you there's nothing dangerous in these mountains?"

The man picked up the knife and tilted it, so he could look at Taz in the reflection of the shiny metal blade.

"Taz, it's better to be safe than sorry, did you bring the compass? We'll need it when we reach the top."

"Yes I did...is that why you invited me to come with you? Just so you could borrow my Uncles compass?" Taz asked.

"It wasn't the only reason." Now the man had a small grin.

"That's rude! Now that I think about it, maybe I don't want to come with you after all. It might be too dangerous for a young orphan like me to climb that mountain. Maybe I'll take this compass back home and let you climb the mountain alone." Taz spoke arrogantly, as he knew he had what the man needed. The young man turned his head from the blade and looked directly at Taz.

"Taz, you're a pretty smart kid, but are you saying you'd rather spend the day helping your Uncle with the chickens?" Taz thought about it for a second, then narrowed his eyes.

"Dragon, you sir, are a tough negotiator. I definitely want to come with you."

"Good! We've got to reach the summit by sundown, so we should get going pretty soon. Did you pack some food?"

"Well duh, what do you think is in my rucksack? Don't worry, we've got enough food to last for days." Taz patted his leather rucksack. "I also have this." Taz reached into his pocket and pulled out a circular piece of metal.

"What is it?" The man examined it closely, studying the strange symbols which were carved into the metallic object.

"It's a gift from my Uncle. He told me I needed to give it to you before you left on your journey." Taz glanced over the man's shoulder. "Is that a new painting Dragon?"

"Actually yes, I've been having some very strange dreams recently. When I wake up, I can't really remember much, except for some moving colors. I thought painting them might help me remember."

"Does it have a name?" Taz walked over to the painting.

"What do you mean?" The man replied.

"Every painting should have a name. Look, the artist used to name his paintings." Taz pointed to a painting of a mountain.

"Mystic Mountain, I'm pretty sure this is the same mountain we're going to climb today."

"Yes, I think you're right. But I can't even think of a name for myself, I don't think I'll be able to name my paintings anytime soon. You can help me name them if you want? But it will have to wait until we get back. We should get going." He stood up and placed a large cloak over his shoulders. Taz stared at the knife hanging from the man's belt.

"Hey Dragon, can I carry the knife?"

"I don't think so Taz, but you can carry my water bottle."

The two headed along the pathway away from the cabin, towards a large mountain in the distance. They wore their cloaks while they traveled. The temperature was quite comfortable, but up the mountain, the air would get considerably cooler. This was the tallest mountain in the area, but still wasn't tall enough to have any snow at the summit. Under his cloak, Taz wore colorful clothes and had a leather rucksack full of supplies. He had spiky hair and wore a pair of goggles like a headband. The young man carried a long wooden stick and walked one step behind Taz. The man had long dark hair and wore simple clothes. He was tall and walked with confidence.

The path they were walking eventually diverged. One way led to Valley Village, which is where Taz lived. They took the other route, towards the foot of the mountain. As they traveled along the path away from the village, the mountain became the focus of their vision. The further they walked, the better they could see the mountain in all of its magnificence.

"So your Uncle, what exactly does he do for a living?" The man asked.

"Well he's a carpenter, and a farmer, and I think he's also a mechanic," Taz replied.

"Hmm, I haven't seen too many vehicles around the village?"

"Like I said, *I think* he's a mechanic."

"Interesting…So how did you get the name Taz, it's pretty unusual?"

"I don't know. I guess it's from my parents. You know, my real parents."

"Yes, I know, you're one of the war orphans from Tiberia." The man softened his voice. "When you think about it, we have a lot in common." Taz stopped and listened to what the man had to say. "I have no memories. I don't know who I am or where I come from. In many ways, I'm a lot like an orphan."

"Taz and Dragon, the orphans from Valley Village!" Taz put his hands on his hips and stuck out his chest. The man smiled back at Taz.

"Taz, you don't need to call me Dragon. I've been thinking about a real name for myself, just in case I never get my memories back."

"What is it?"

"If you're lucky I'll tell you later. We've got to keep going."

They carried on walking along the path until they reached the foot of the mountain. The stream which flowed down the side of the artist's cabin was now a strong river. The water crashed into large rocks and splashed rather loudly. The man looked at the river and thought about his past, which alluded him.

The path up the mountain was steep, but no actual climbing

was needed to reach the summit. You could reach the top within a day if you didn't take too many breaks. This day was perfect for a hike. Light, fluffy clouds scattered across the clear blue skies made the mountain look simply spectacular. Just like in the artist's painting.

The two travellers looked up at the mountain in awe. It was much bigger than it had looked from a distance. The man felt something twitching in his stomach. As he gazed at the summit, the feeling grew stronger. This was the same feeling that gave him the idea to climb the mountain in the first place. He felt it every time he looked at the mountain from the artist's cabin. He couldn't describe it in words. It felt like his destiny was at the top of this mountain, waiting for him. It was as if getting to the top was more important than anything else. It was all he thought about. He was convinced this was his destiny.

They walked up the side of the mountain. Now the young man led the way and Taz followed. A large black bird swooped through the air in their vicinity. It was hunting. It looked down at the grass for any mice or creature, which might have been foolish enough to be out in the open on such a clear day. Unfortunately for the hunter, the sound of footsteps were enough to make sure the area was all clear. Frustrated, the bird swooped down and let out a loud cry to warn the two trespassers out of its territory. The young man froze with his hand on the knife, keeping full eye contact with the bird as it flew away.

"Good thing you brought it!" Taz yelled in excitement.

"Calm down Taz, let's keep going."

"Can we stop to eat something? All this walking is making me hungry,"

"Let's get over that ridge and then take a short break."

About an hour later, they deviated from the trail and found a grassy area on the side of the mountain. There were some rocks, which served as chairs, while they sat and ate their lunch. Taz let out a small groan as he took off his rucksack. The young man leaned his wooden stick against one of the rocks and took a seat facing the valley from where they came.

"Do you still need the stick?" Taz asked.

"No, I'm just used to the feel of it. I can walk totally fine without it. Look, you can see the village." The man gazed at the landscape.

"Oh yeah, is that why you wanted to come here? To look at Valley Village?"

"Not exactly, I can't really explain it. Every morning when I wake up, I look at this mountain. Recently, I've felt the urge to climb it. I guess I want to see what's at the top. Do you believe in destiny, Taz?"

"I don't know, I never really thought about it," Taz spoke halfheartedly, as he unbuckled his rucksack.

"I can't explain it Taz. There's something drawing me to the top of this mountain."

"Do you want an avocado from my Uncles garden?" Taz offered a small green fruit to the man.

"...that sounds good, thanks Taz."

The two ate in silence. A small breeze kept the air feeling fresh and cool. Taz finished much quicker than the man and pulled out an object from his rucksack. He held it in both hands, turning it upside down, shaking it, and holding it to his ear.

"What's that?" The man asked.

"It's a puzzle, I got it from Sister Mary." Taz jammed his fingers into it. "There's a special trick to opening the lock. None of the other kids at school could figure it out. The only clue is this red dot on the side. I'm going to find the solution by the time we return to the village. Sister Mary will be so impressed. I bet she'll even give me a kiss."

"Taz, you're full of surprises. But aren't you a little young for that sort of stuff?"

"I'm eleven, and Sister Mary is only a few years older."

"She's nineteen." The young man pointed out.

"How do you know that!? I hope you're not thinking of trying to steal my girl? In case you didn't realize, there are limited options in such a small village. I'm planning ahead. Sister Mary is the best looking girl in the whole of Valley Village,and I can't have you messing everything up."

"You don't need to worry about me. But I heard from one of the villagers that you might have some competition from the blacksmith's apprentice. I think his name is Robert."

"Rob?! That guy is a total loser. Sister Mary would never be with him. No way! When I get back to the village, I'm going to tell Rob to stay away from my girl!"

"Wow Taz, I think you're really in love. Just be careful. I'm sure you'll get over her, eventually."

"Like you know anything about girls, you don't even have memories."

"I suppose you're right. I have an idea. As an added incentive, if you get that puzzle open, I'll tell you my new name. Now let's pack up and go." They walked back towards the path that led up the mountain.

"What about your walking stick?" Taz asked.

"I don't need it anymore, today is a new beginning."

The further they hiked, the less worn the path became. Halfway up the mountain, their pace slowed, as the air got a little thinner and the temperature fell. As the day grew older, the bright sun slowly faded away. Luckily for the two explorers, Taz's Uncle was right, there was nothing too dangerous up the mountain. They progressed uninterrupted for a few more hours. They gradually reached the point where they could see the other side of the valley.

The young man could feel it, they were close to something. There really was something mysterious about this mountain. Something was calling him to reach the summit. But what could it be? It almost felt like a sense of Déjà vu for the man. But is that even possible? For someone who's lost their memories. Who knows? But one thing was certain, the young man had to reach the top and find out.

One year ago, the man awoke in Valley Village. He was disoriented and severely injured. He had no memory of who he was or where he came from. One of the villagers found him washed up on the shores of Lyme Cove, about ten miles from the village. They carried him on the back of their trailer to the village medical station, where he was treated for his injuries. Even with villages limited equipment, the doctor stabilized his condition. Sister Mary was left to watch over him, while he lay unconscious for many days. Mary was a nurse in training. She grew up in the village and when she wasn't at medical station, she would help at the local school and orphanage.

Although she wasn't really qualified, she tried to investigate where this man could have possibly come from and also the cause of his injuries. He had several lacerations down the left side of his body. Based on the position of the cuts, she hypothesized that he could have been near an explosion. He most likely turned sideways and used his left arm to shield his face from the blast. She also surmised, that because the sea at Lyme Cove is on the southern coast of Middle Continent, it's possible, however unlikely, that he came from Southern Continent. Her final conclusion was that the most probable explanation, would have been some sort of accident at sea. For example, an explosion on board of a ship. Although not completely correct, some aspects of Mary's conclusions were surprisingly accurate.

When he finally awoke, he was greeted by Sister Mary and the hospital staff. When he was strong enough to walk they showed him around the village. He met Taz's Uncle, who offered to make him a walking stick to help him move around more freely. It was then that Taz's Uncle gave him the nickname 'Buck'. Buck was somewhat of a celebrity in the village. The mysterious man with no past who appeared out of nowhere. After a few days, when he was well enough to leave the medical station, Taz's Uncle suggested he live in the artist's cabin. He thought a calm environment might help his mind recover from whatever had caused him to lose his memories. Mary had very intelligently concluded, that his memory loss was not related to his physical injuries. He had suffered no apparent head trauma. It was possibly stress related. The villagers gathered some supplies for Buck and left him alone to live in the cabin.

He would occasionally come back to visit the village. It was only a half mile walk. The villagers were always excited to see Buck, especially Taz. There wasn't much excitement in Valley Village. It was a peaceful place with only about five hundred people. Most of the adults were craftsmen and farmers. There wasn't much of an economy and very seldom would people visit from other places. A lot of the younger adults would leave the village to travel to larger towns or cities in search of jobs. That meant most of the remaining population were very old or very young.

The buildings were mostly simple wooden structures. There were a few larger community properties, such as the medical center, a school, and a library. An old farm house was converted into an orphanage, to give shelter to war orphans, like Taz. Since the War of Tiberia, surrounding regions were called upon to help resettle the mass quantities of refugees and orphans. Some towns and cities rejected the request. Valley Village was happy to do what it could to help with the crises.

Buck would spend most of his time exploring the surrounding valley and observing the wildlife. He liked to sit in the grass next to the cabin and watch the stream as it flowed along the muddy bank. He thought about how the stream must have been there for thousands of years. It could only flow along a single path that occurred naturally. No matter how much the water may have tried, it could never deviate away from the path it was given. That was nature. That was the natural course and destiny for the stream. But what was his destiny?

Back on the mountain, they approached the summit and made it in good time. There was still an hour of sunlight left. As they got closer, the man could feel something inside his stomach making him feel nervous and excited. He breathed heavy. With every footstep his chest pounded harder and harder. This was it. This is what he had been looking for. Secretly, he was hoping it would trigger the return of his memories. But even if it didn't, he knew coming here would give him something. He just didn't know what it could be.

The wind blew fairly hard at the top of the mountain. It was cold, but not uncomfortable. The two could easily spend the night at the top, but it wasn't night time just yet. As they reached their goal, they could hear some unusual noises coming from over a ridge. It sounded like some sort of percussion. Something tapping quickly against the rocky path at an irregular pace. As they got a little closer, they could hear snarling. It sounded like some sort of wild animal. What could it be?

"What the hell is that noise?" Taz exclaimed.

"Taz, shut up and tread carefully. At the first sign of trouble, run down the mountain as fast as you can and don't stop until you're back at the village." The man removed the knife from his belt. They crept up the mountain and perched on a ledge. Now they could see where the noises were coming from.

"Those are wild dogs," Taz whispered. "They're probably fighting over territory, I learned about it at school. Wild animals fight each other for land."

"It's not just wild animals who fight each other for land, Taz. As long as it's only the two of them, they shouldn't be any risk to us. But if there's a full pack, we might have to cut this trip short. I wouldn't like to be alone up a mountain with a whole bunch of them." The wild dogs in this area were fairly small. They mostly ate vegetation and occasionally would hunt smaller animals.

"I guess my Uncle was wrong," Taz whispered.

"He wasn't wrong, this type of wild dog wouldn't normally be this high up the mountain. They live down in the forests. There must be something up here, which drew them away from their natural habitat. *Could it be the same thing which drew me to this mountain?*"

The two dogs circled each other menacingly. They curled their upper lips as high as possible to show their teeth to their opponent. They would lunge at each other and grapple with their front legs, each trying to get the upper hand. Every attack was aimed at the opponents neck. The two dogs were very different. One was a deep burgundy, with shiny fur, and a large snout. He was more aggressive and the larger of the two. He had the upper hand in the fight. The smaller dog was a slightly chubby female. She was unusually colored, with black and gray spots. She had rough, spiky fur, and rich blue eyes. Her snout was much smaller and not really made for fighting. Although she wanted to exert her dominance, at this point, she was just fighting to survive.

The young man froze, staring at the dueling dogs. He felt emotions, which somehow reminded him of his past. His hands began to tremble. The two dogs seemed to move in slow motion, as images flashed in his mind from another lifetime. As confusing as it might have seemed, something deep within him understood perfectly. Without even realizing, he slowly nodded his head. Then something drew his attention from the fight.

He looked out into the distant landscape from above the mountain. From this height, he could see for miles. He looked north and took a deep breath. The man could feel there was going to be some sort of battle in his future. Some inescapable conflict. He was going to have to fight someone or something. Whatever it was, it was something he couldn't avoid. It was his destiny. As he looked to the north again, his moment of clarity was broken.

The two dogs circled each other one last time. They leaped forward with their front legs extended and jaws wide open. The male dog pinned the female down and gripped her paw in his mouth. He bit down hard and she howled in pain. He shook his mouth with her paw clamped in his jaw, then released his grip, and went for the kill.

"The brown one is going to eat the fat one," Taz whispered.

"Not if I can help it!" Without thinking, the man jumped down from the ledge and charged towards the wild dogs. He yelled at the male aggressor to back away and stood over the prone female. The male dog stepped back begrudgingly and growled angrily at the human. Sensing he couldn't win two fights, the ferocious male turned around and ran down the side of the mountain.

The female dog lay still, but looked up at the man. She was panting with her tongue hanging out the side of her mouth. She lay defeated. The man knelt down slowly and placed his hand on her chest, as it quickly moved up and down. The dog felt uncomfortable and untrusting of this stranger. But she was too scared and unable to react. The man slowly moved his hand and rubbed her side.

"Don't be frightened my little friend." The man tried to sound as unthreatening as possible.

For a brief moment, she felt safe and immediately leaped to her feet and ran off in the opposite direction from the male dog who attacked her. She limped and ran much slower than she normally could, but within seconds, she vanished out of sight.

"*Oh well, I tried.* Come on, it's safe! This will make a good spot for our camp." He waived Taz down from the ledge.

"Are you crazy?! That dog might have bit you!"

"She wouldn't have, I could feel it."

Taz climbed down from the ledge and brushed off some dirt from his knees. He walked towards the man cautiously, but was trying to act unafraid. After looking around for any other wild animals, he slid off his rucksack and unpacked his supplies. The two could finally look around and take in the amazing views of the surrounding landscape. There was just enough sunlight left.

It was mostly grassy plains with rocky hills and small rivers which flowed across the land. In the opposite direction, they could see the southern coast of Middle Continent and Lyme Cove. Cliffs overlooked the sandy beach and the deep blue sea sparkled in the sunset.

The man spent some time looking in each direction. He looked for any landmark, which might hold some hidden meaning. Anything, which might trigger the return of his memories, but there was nothing. He let out a slow breath of disappointment.

"Taz, get everything setup. I'm going to get some firewood. Don't worry, I won't go far."

"Don't bother, I brought a portable fire generator." Taz reached into his rucksack looking for the device.

"Really?" The man was genuinely surprised.

"I'm way smarter than you give me credit for, at least one of us planned ahead. We've got sandwiches for dinner. Let's see what my Uncle put in them." Taz pulled out some sandwiches from his bag and sniffed them, not noticing what was behind him.

"Taz, walk towards me slowly. Leave your bag where it is and don't make any sudden movements."

"Ok, I'm scared, what's going on?" Taz froze.

"Don't worry, everything's fine." The man waived Taz towards him calmly. Taz walked slowly, then turned to look what was behind him. He jumped back and hid behind the man. The wounded female dog walked slowly towards Taz's rucksack. She maintained constant eye contact with the two humans, as she shoved her snout into the bag and rummaged through its contents.

"Do something!" Taz whispered loudly.

"It's ok, she's just hungry."

"But that's my sandwich!"

The man walked slowly towards the female dog and stopped about ten feet away. He knelt down and stuck his hand out. She took her head out of the bag and stared directly at him. She lifted her front paw and timidly took a step towards him.

"That's it, come on." He said softly.

The dog took another step and with a little encouragement, moved close enough to sniff the back of his hand. After two or three sniffs, she stuck her tongue out and licked his hand briefly. It was enough to communicate a message of peace. The man lifted his hand and placed it on top of the dogs head. He slowly stroked her face and while still maintaining eye contact, she licked his hand again.

"I think she likes you," Taz said excitingly. "Can I try?"

"Sure, just stay calm and walk towards us slowly."

Taz approached the dog. He stuck his hand out and rubbed her back. She pointed her face down and looked up at the two of them, wagging her tail in excitement.

"Taz, let's get that fire going. It looks like we're going to have a guard dog to keep us safe tonight."

"I don't think she's going to keep us safe from very much, but she's cute though." Taz knelt down and rubbed her cheeks.

"She sure is." The man pulled out some meat from one of the sandwiches and offered it to her. There was no doubt that she trusted him now. Taz quickly started the fire and although she was startled at first, the warmth drew her close. The three sat around the small fluorescent flame and ate their sandwiches.

"Let's call her Moja," the man said.

"Moja? Where did you get that from?"

"I just thought of it. It came to me in the moment." He patted her on the back.

"This is for you, Moja." Taz handed her the crusts from his sandwich. She loved the heat from the fire and lay as close as she could. She gently chewed the scrap of bread, while Taz rubbed her ears. The man couldn't help but smile at the two of them. Taz wiped the crumbs from his lap, then pulled out the puzzle from his bag. He held it up and looked at it from different angles. After pausing for a moment and lifting his eyebrow, he held the puzzle in front of Moja's nose so she could sniff it. She didn't know the solution either. Taz sighed and went back to trying different combinations.

"What the hell is that?!" Taz looked closely at the puzzle. There were faint arrows appearing on the side. "Is that it?" He pulled individual pieces in the direction of the arrows and it slid open with ease. "Yes, I did it!" He jumped up and presented the completed puzzle to the man. "Sister Mary is going to be so impressed and now you have to tell me your name!" The man took the puzzle from Taz and examined it.

"The heat from the fire must have made the arrows appear. That's the meaning of the red dot and the secret to this puzzle. Very clever, Taz. Well done."

"That's right, now tell me!"

"Alright, until I get my memories back, my name will be Hunter."

"That's so cool. Two names in one day, Moja and Hunter. You're doing good!"

"I know, maybe I'll even be able to name some of my paintings when we get back." Hunter laughed slightly.

Shortly after eating, Hunter lay on the ground and listened to Taz and Moja while they both snored loudly. He stared at the flame as it flickered in the dead of night. Unsure of what he would do next, he closed his eyes.

"Why did I come here? Was it to meet Moja? Could she hold some secret answer? That couldn't be it. There's something up here that can help me, I know it, I feel it. Maybe I'll have to wait for the right conditions for the solution to present itself. Just like Taz's puzzle."

Hunter entered a deep sleep and began to see images in his mind. He experienced these visions frequently. They were much more than just dreams. A blue light danced around a black canvas, then made a sphere in the center of his vision. It rotated slowly and calmly. In the very center of the sphere, a red light emerged, bleeding outwards towards the edge. The blue light became engulfed in red flames and started to burn intensely. Hunter could feel the heat within his dream. A black crow swooped down and grabbed the sphere in its razor sharp talons. The sphere shattered, like glass, into hundreds of pieces.

Out of the black, two piercing red eyes appeared. They looked directly into Hunters' soul. He couldn't breathe. He was paralyzed. There was no escape from the eyes of the devil. His body trembled in fear as the eyes grew closer. They exploded into a giant flash of Alizerin Crimson. As the smoke cleared, he could see the outline of the devil's face burned into the canvas. It was the face of pure evil, his nemesis. At that same moment, a giant sword thrust through the canvas and cut a gapping hole. A hand reached out through the gap. It was covered in metallic armor, like a knight's gauntlet. Hunter couldn't see who the hand belonged to, but for some reason he couldn't explain, he took the hand and held it in his own. He immediately awoke on top of the mountain.

The night air was silent. Taz and Moja were still fast asleep. Hunter walked towards the edge of the mountain. Out of the black night sky, a soft Phthalo Blue light appeared from the heavens. It shined in the distance, pointing towards an area far in the west. He finally found what he was looking for. Hunter stared at the blue light, then used the compass, to mark the direction it was pointing.

2 TECH CITY

Tech City, Middle Continent
Day 5 Month 2 Year 2037

Far away from Valley Village, stood a futuristic urban metropolis known as Tech City. Skyscrapers pierced the sky and the cityscape was a tribute to the technological advancements of mankind. Tech City wasn't an old place. In fact, it was the youngest city on the planet of Eros. It had been meticulously planned from inception and executed to perfection. A huge artificial lake completely surrounded the city. From a great distance, the lake resembled a moat protecting a medieval castle. The water was always perfectly still with artificial ripples created at regular intervals. At night, underwater lights would create a soft,white glow. It truly looked like a city from the future. Four bridges were built over the water to access the city. The bridges pointed north, south, east, and west. The city stood on an island in the center, and from above, Tech City looked like a giant target.

From street level all you could see in any direction were neon lights, people, advertisements, vehicles, and gigantic buildings. If you looked up the skyscrapers were so tall that you could barely see the sky. The skyscrapers were covered in huge panes of glass, which reflected the lights from the city streets. There was constant energy and stimulation for the senses. The exact opposite from Valley Village.

The southern bridge leading into the city was strangely quiet on this summer evening. Daylight was fading away, as the occasional vehicle drifted along the highway. South Bridge was the least busy of the four bridges leading into Tech City, especially later in the day. To the south, there were only small towns and no areas of large population. South Bridge could be considered one of the least interesting parts of Tech City. Except today, two people were walking across towards the city center.

A tall man walked with a shorter boy at his side. The boy held a piece of rope wrapped around a dog's neck using it as a leash. The three of them walked steadily towards the city, as the cityscape burned in the horizon in front of the setting Sun.

"Taz let's walk a bit faster. I want to get there before the shops close."

"Don't worry Hunter, we've got plenty of time. Also, Moja's paw has started to hurt her again. She's limping a little bit."

"Damn, I thought it had healed. I've got some of Mary's cream in my bag. When we get to the city we can put some more on her paw." Hunter took a piece of paper out from his pocket.

"I still can't believe how huge this place is. Do you really think we'll find that store?" Taz looked at the cityscape in awe. He'd never seen anything like it.

"According to the truck driver's directions, it's right on the other side of this bridge. It should be there as soon as we enter the city limit." Hunter listened to the city noises, which echoed across the water beneath him. It sounded so foreign and unusual to him.

"I wish he could have driven us all the way there. This bridge must be twenty miles long. My legs are killing me." Taz moaned.

"Taz, we're pretty lucky he drove us as far as he did. I don't think it's far now. Look at that sign."

WELCOME TO TECH CITY
WHERE DREAMS MEET REALITY
POPULATION 15,000,000

The three approached the end of South Bridge and stood at the outskirts of Tech City. There were mostly industrial buildings and a few cars driving through the streets. On the corner near the end of the bridge was a small commercial area with a few stores and a café. It was a place catered for travelers entering or leaving the city. One store was of great importance. It had a large red neon sign, which read 'Lizzy's Pet Supplies'.

"Just like the truck driver said. I'm sure they'll have what we're looking for. Let me check if we can bring Moja inside."

Hunter entered the store, while Taz stood outside with Moja. He rubbed her ears as she sat, patiently waiting. She was surprisingly well behaved for a wild dog. That was, until she was startled by a fast moving car, which came too close. She lunged forward and barked loudly at the vehicle, as Taz tried with all his strength to hold her steady.

"Moja, shut up! It's just a car." Taz pulled her back towards him.

"Taz it's ok, bring her in." Hunter waved them into the store. They immediately started looking at the different collars and leashes available.

"I don't see why we have to buy her a collar, this rope is doing just fine." Taz said.

"I know Taz, but I don't want to take any chances. If she has a nice collar, then I don't think anyone will suspect she's actually a wild dog." Moja stood inquisitively, looking at the leashes. She had her mouth open with her tongue slightly hanging out. She was panting just a little a bit, which made it look like she was smiling. "What about this one?" Hunter asked.

"It's bright pink with sparkles." Taz said, very unimpressed.

"She's a girl. I think it's perfect. Look how cute she looks." Hunter held it against Moja's neck. She sniffed it and her tail started wagging. She gripped it in her mouth and started tugging it from Hunter's hand.

"It's not a toy, Moja." Hunter pulled it from her mouth and picked up the matching leash. He proceeded to the cashier to pay for the items.

"A fine choice, sir. What brings you to Tech City?" The cashier spoke with a thick accent. Before Hunter could answer, Taz interrupted.

"Some creepy guy in a black cloak told us to come here. We're looking for something important. Is there anywhere to eat around here?"

"Hmm, there's a café just opposite," the cashier replied.

"Thanks for your help." Hunter smiled, then firmly put his hand on Taz's back and pushed him out of the store. "Taz, it's not a good idea to tell people why we're here. I don't want to make people suspicious."

"How are we going to find what we're looking for unless we ask questions? The man in black didn't give us much of a description of what we're looking for."

"Taz, don't worry, we'll find it. I'm certain." Hunter put the new collar on Moja and handed the leash to Taz. Moja felt proud to have such a fancy looking collar. She was still a little chubby, but had a sense of elegance in the way she posed. She stood next to Taz, loyally waiting for their next move. They walked over to the café and sat down outside.

"This is the plan. Let's eat something and then go to the hotel the truck driver suggested, the 'Dolphin Inn'. We should possibly think about looking for work. We have enough cash to last for a short time, but we don't know how long we're going to be here."

"I wish I didn't have to sell my treasure," Taz sighed.

"Taz, you should never have taken that jewel from the temple. But at least now we don't have to worry about money. I still can't believe that jeweler paid us as much as he did."

"I was going to give it to Sister Mary." Taz pouted his lips, as the waitress served them a bowl of rice noodles with catula sprouts. She even poured some water into a bowl for Moja. Catula is a green vegetable, which grows in this part of Middle Continent. It's a local delicacy in Tech City and surrounding regions. Taz definitely did not like its unusual sour taste.

"Ugh, this is gross." Taz said.

"It's a bit strange, but I sort of like it." Hunter tasted a small piece of catula sprout.

"You can finish mine." Taz pushed his bowl towards Hunter.

After their small meal, they walked a short distance to the Dolphin Inn. As you might expect, a neon sign with a dolphin hung at the entrance. Truck drivers frequented this place because it was much cheaper than the high priced accommodation in the city center. The rooms were simple, but served their purpose. Except for a few bars and convenience stores, they were surrounded by mostly factories and large storage buildings. Hunter and Taz entered the small reception in front of the hotel. A tall skinny receptionist stood behind the counter, silently smoking a cigarette. He completely ignored the new arrivals.

"Good evening, we would like a room with two separate beds." Hunter tried to sound as friendly possible. The reception took a slow puff from his cigarette before replying.

"It's fifty woolongs a night, plus twenty-five deposit for the dog."

"That sounds great, we're might be here a long time, is that alright?"

"As long as you pay, you can stay for as long as you want, pal." The receptionist replied.

Hunter handed the receptionist some cash, who in turn, handed Hunter the keys to room 101. They left the reception and entered the small, but affordable room. It had two beds, a television, a small table, and a bathroom. It was everything they needed and nothing more.

"Well, I'm beat, time for bed." Taz jumped onto one of the two beds. Moja sniffed every corner of the room and examined her new surroundings.

"Not so fast Taz. We need to take Moja on a short walk before we got to sleep. I don't want her making a mess on the carpet like she did at your Uncles house. Otherwise we'll lose our deposit. But if you're really tired, I can take her by myself."

"No way, I wanna see the city." Taz stood back up.

"We're not going into the city center. We're just going to walk around this area. We're right on the outskirts, so we can walk along the water. I saw some docks on the walk over here, which might be interesting to take a look at."

Hunter and Taz took Moja by her new leash and walked around the industrial area on the southern side of Tech City. It was now late in the evening and the city looked even more exciting at night. Even though they were on the outskirts, they could feel the energy coming from the city center. The neon lights illuminated the night sky. They were all were excited by the thought of exploring this urban metropolis, including Moja.

They walked around one of the docks and looked at the water as it rippled like a metronome. There was no one around at this time of night.

"Hunter, have you ever seen a city like this?" Taz asked.

"No, at least, I don't think I have. What about you? Does it remind you of Tiberia?"

"I don't remember much about my life in Tiberia. I just remember little snippets, like a picture puzzle with some pieces missing. I can't even remember what my parents looked like. It's all just a distant memory."

Before Hunter could reply, a loud bang exploded in the near distance. Hunter and Taz looked at each other confused. They stood completely still and then Hunter realized what they had heard.

"Taz, give me Moja's leash and follow me, it's not safe around here."

They crouched behind a stack of wooden crates and peeked through a small gap. It was completely silent. Moja made small muffled noises, as Hunter held her mouth shut. Hunter looked over the crates and saw a man dressed in a black suit dragging a body across the dock towards the water. The man pushed the body over the edge and hastily walked away. A car started in distance and then there was silence again.

Hunter had no idea what he had just witnessed. It all happened so quickly. He looked at Taz, but couldn't say a word. He was completely speechless. Hunter placed his hand on Taz's shoulder and gave him a signal to stay still. He handed Taz Moja's leash and stood up slowly. After looking around in every direction, he cautiously stepped out from behind the crates. Before he could check the area was safe, Moja let out a loud succession of barks and howls. Taz tried to hold her mouth, but it was too late, anyone in the area would have heard her. Luckily for the three of them, no one was around. Hunter slowly walked towards the edge of the dock.

"Oh shit!" Taz exclaimed.

"Taz, what are you doing? You were meant to stay behind the crates."

"Sorry, I wanted to see for myself." They looked down into the water. In the glow of the underwater lighting, they could see the silhouette of a body.

"We need to leave right now." Hunter said.

They hastily left the dock and after a short distance, saw a black sports car with the driver's door wide open. It had been abandoned. Taz and Hunter looked up and down the empty street. They approached the car very slowly and checked there was absolutely no one around.

"Could this have been the dead guy's car?" Taz said, as he looked through the rear window. Hunter climbed inside the driver's seat. He leaned over and tried to open the glove box, but it was locked.

"You might want to try these." Taz said, as he handed him a set of keys.

"Where did you get those?" Hunter asked.

"I found them on the ground right here, Moja was sniffing them." Hunter opened the glove box and took out all of its contents. There were three items; an address, written on a scrap piece of paper, a business card for the 'Tech City Piano Bar', and a strange looking key. On the key was a double sided keyring. One side said 'A9', on the other, '1853'. The numbers didn't mean anything to Hunter. Taz opened the trunk, but there was nothing inside, except a black leather jacket with empty pockets. Hunter got out of the car and made a bold decision.

"Taz, we need to find out who that man was and why he was killed. I'm not sure if it's connected to the reason why we came here, but I would like to find out."

"Are you sure that's a good idea?" Taz was hesitant, as he thought about the man in the water."

"Taz trust me, we're not going to do anything dangerous. I promised your Uncle I'd keep you safe."

"Alright. Solving a murder does sound like fun."

"We're also taking this car."

"Um Hunter, are you sure that's a good idea? Do you even know how to drive?"

"I don't know, lets find out." Hunter examined the dashboard. He put his hands on the steering wheel and the car started automatically. Taz put Moja on the back seat and then sat next to Hunter. Hunter drove slowly and carefully back to the Dolphin Inn. When they arrived, the receptionist walked up to the car.

"Nice vehicle, it's another twenty woolongs for a parking pass." The receptionist held out his hand and Hunter gave him the cash. Hunter took the three items from the glove box to their room, so he could examine them further. Although their adrenaline was still pumping, they were exhausted from their journey to Tech City. They fell asleep easily and there were no dreams for Hunter that night.

The next morning, Taz woke up with Moja sleeping at the foot of his bed. Hunter was already awake, looking at the clues from the glove box. Just like when he lived in the artist's cabin, he started the day with a cup of fresh coffee.

"Good morning Taz, I have good news. We're going into the city center today."

"That's great," Taz yawned. "What are were going to do?"

"We're going to visit this address." Hunter held up the scrap piece of paper.

"Ok, but first I need to take a quick shower. I don't think I washed since we left Valley Village. What about Moja? Is she coming?"

"I think we should leave her here. I just put some cream on her paw and she could use some rest. I gave her a nice walk this morning. It's funny, I went back to the docks and it was full of workers. In the day light, you can't see anything in the water. You'd never guess there was a murder there last night."

"Hunter, what about the police? Shouldn't we tell them?"

"We probably should… but seeing as we drove away in the dead man's car, we might become their prime suspects. Someone will eventually find the body. When that happens, we can go to the police and explain what happened. First, I want to investigate myself."

They left Moja sleeping on Taz's bed and drove off towards the center of Tech City. Even though the city was densely populated, there was hardly ever any traffic. The cities infrastructure was perfectly planned to avoid congestion. You could drive from one side of the city to the other within thirty minutes, even at rush hour. As they drove through the streets, Taz looked out of the window in awe at all of the neon signs. He'd never seen anything so bright and vibrant. It was like a different planet compared to Valley Village. As they approached the city center, Taz stared up at the skyscrapers.

"This is it." Hunter pulled the car in front of a very tall apartment building. "We want apartment 307. I guess we just knock on the door and see what happens." Hunter and Taz entered the building. Taz shrugged his shoulders at the stylish decorations, as they walked through the lobby. During the elevator ride up to the thirtieth floor, Hunter realized he might be making a big mistake.

"Taz, this could be a potentially dangerous situation. Maybe you should wait in the car."

"I'll be alright, I've got your knife in my jacket pocket."

"Are you crazy?! Taz, you can't carry a weapon in public. This isn't Valley Village. They have strict laws in cities like this."

"Hunter, chill out man, no one will ever know I have it."

On the thirtieth floor, they looked through the corridor until they found the correct apartment. Hunter nervously looked at

Taz for a short moment, then knocked on the door. To his relief, a woman in her forties answered.

"How may I help you?" She asked timidly. Hunter had no idea of what he was going to say, but tried to explain the situation.

"Good morning, madam. Ugh, this is going to sound very strange. We recently found an abandoned car and inside the glove box was a piece of paper with your address on it." The lady looked at Hunter slightly confused and then suspiciously peered at Taz, not saying a word. "We were hoping you might know who the car belongs to." After another moment's silence, she finally replied.

"...you better come inside." She invited them to sit down in her well-furnished living room. "May I see the piece of paper?" Hunter pulled it out from his pocket and handed it to her. "This is my handwriting...was it a black sports car?"

"Yes, it was," Hunter replied.

"The car belongs to a private investigator. His name is Michael Paris. I hired him to look into my son's case. So you've found his car? That's strange."

"Well, we think he might have been murdered..." Hunter wasn't sure if he should have revealed this piece of information.

"Murdered?! That's terrible, I knew there was something odd about this whole situation. Do you think his murder is somehow related to my son's disappearance? My son, could he also have been murdered?" A tear rolled down her face, as she held her forehead.

"Madam, I'm sorry, we don't know anything about your son. We just wanted to know more about the car we found and identify its owner."

"Why? Why do you care about this car? Are you private investigators as well? Can you help me find my son?" Her frantic voice was filled with desperation and sorrow. "I'm sorry, it's been a difficult time for me."

"There's no need to apologize. Can you tell us about your son? What happened?"

"My son went missing about six months ago. The police weren't very helpful, so I hired an investigator." Hunter glanced over her shoulder at a photo of the lady's son, hanging on the wall. "His name is Max. He's twelve years old. He started working at a comic book store a few weeks before he disappeared. It was just a small job for after school. He went to work one day and never came home. The store said he left at his usual time. He was probably abducted on his way home. I don't know. The police just didn't seem interested. I'd almost given up hope. Then Michael Paris contacted me, saying he'd heard about my case and offered to help. I was so grateful. It's been so long. I've started to accept the fact he might be gone forever, but I just want to know what happened to him."

Hunter looked at the picture of Max again and couldn't help but think that Taz was almost the same age.

"Maybe we can help you find your son?" Hunter said.

"Really?" The woman replied.

"We came to Tech City because someone told us we would find something. Something important. I supposed we are investigators, in a way. We just didn't know what we were supposed to investigate, until now. Last night, a man was murdered. We saw his body thrown into the water, on the outskirts of Tech City. That man was probably Michael Paris.

We found his car and in the glove box was your address, which led us to you. I don't think this is a coincidence. I think this is what we were supposed to find in Tech City. We're supposed to find your son."

Even though she thought he sounded a little crazy and didn't fully understand his story, Hunters words filled the woman with optimism.

"I can't believe you want to help me. I'm so grateful." She said.

"We will do our best." Hunter smiled at her, then Taz interjected himself into the conversation.

"When you say you hired Michael Paris. Does that mean there was some sort of payment involved?"

"Please excuse my little friend." Hunter used his facial expression to keep Taz quiet.

"No, it's quite alright. I will cover all of your expenses and pay you anything you want, just please help me." The woman replied.

"I need to know the name of the comic book store. Also, have you ever heard of the Tech City Piano Bar?" Hunter asked.

"The store is called 'Big World Comics', the manager's name is Steve. I've never heard of the piano bar."

"Thank you for the information. We'll be in touch as soon as we find anything useful. By the way, what's your name?"

"Katrin. Katrin Fielder." She replied.

Hunter and Taz left the apartment and took the elevator

back down to the ground floor.

"I guess now we don't need to look for work?" Taz said arrogantly. Hunter looked at him and raised his eyebrow.

"Taz, as I've said before, you're a very smart kid."

As they exited the building and were about to climb inside the black sports car, Katrin Fielder came running out of the lobby and called out.

"Excuse me, there's something else I forgot to tell you!" She noticed the car. "Isn't this Michael Paris' car, you took it?!?"

"Yes we did…" Hunter didn't know what else to say.

"It doesn't matter. I just wanted to tell you something else. When I met with Michael Paris to discuss my son's case, he asked me about something called 'Project Overlord'. I have no idea what it is, but it might help with your investigation."

"Project Overlord." Hunter wrote it down. "Thanks, we'll keep it in mind." Katrin watched them drive away and couldn't help but think that Hunter and Taz were a bit of an odd couple.

Along the way, they stopped at a newsstand. Hunter stepped out of the car, leaving Taz in the passenger seat. He bought a telephone directory and some snacks. He noticed a blue diagram pinned up behind the cashier.

"What's that?" Hunter asked.

"It's a blueprint of the construction plans of Tech City. They make a great souvenir. You want one?" The cashier replied.

"Construction plans?"

"You're not from around here, are you? Tech City is famous because of its perfect street design. Everything you see around you is drawn on these plans. They're only fifteen woolongs."

"Maybe some other time, thanks." As Hunter handed the cashier the money, he saw a group of three children sitting on the pavement next to the street vendor. They were war orphans from Tiberia, just like Taz. They wore tatty clothes and begged for money. They had no place in society. All they had was each other. They were lost children.

Hunter looked at the three of them and then looked at Taz, sitting in the car. He was glad Taz had been lucky enough to end up in a place like Valley Village. A place where orphans could be given a better chance at a new life. Not all the orphans from Tiberia were as lucky. Hunter gave the three children some money, then they ran off through the streets of Tech City. As they drove back to the Dolphin Inn, Taz continued to stare out of the window at the gigantic buildings and the fluorescent advertisements for the whole journey.

When they got back, Moja stood up from the bed where she had been sleeping. She stretched her front legs and yawned. Her tongue extended far from her mouth, as she wagged her tail at the sight of her friends. She jumped down, then ran over to Hunter and Taz.

"See, she slept the whole time we were gone." Hunter handed her a treat. Taz and Hunter stood over the small table, looking at the clues from their investigation. Moja sat staring up at them, wagging her tail.

"So to recap. Our initial goal of finding the identity of the man who was dumped into the water has been solved. The man was Michael Paris, a private investigator who was investigating the disappearance of a twelve-year-old boy called Max. We still don't know who murdered Michael Paris or why. We also have a new mission, to find out what happened to Max."

"We've been here less than twenty four hours and you've managed to turn our original, simple, goal of finding some information into a missing person and murder investigation. Oh, and we're probably going to be wanted by the police as soon as they find Michael Paris' body. Good job Hunter. I guess I won't be doing much sightseeing on this trip."

"Taz, I'm sorry. Bear with me. This will all work itself out, I know it."

"It's fine, but just so you know, I'm keeping all of the payment from Max's mother for myself." Taz clicked his fingers and pointed at Hunter.

"It's a deal." Hunter clicked his fingers back at Taz. "Of the three clues from Michael Paris' glove box, there are two more we need to investigate. Taz, your job is to figure out what this key is for. I want you to go through this phone book and call every bank you can find. Ask them if they keep safety deposit boxes and tell them the numbers on the keyring. Hopefully one will match. I'm going to visit the Tech City Piano Bar. You're definitely too young for a place like that, so I'll go alone. You can keep an eye on Moja here at the hotel and please stay out of trouble."

"You're seriously not going to let me come with you? You're going to make me stay in the hotel, while you explore the city?"

"You'll get your chance tomorrow. You're going to go to that comic book store and ask for a job. Maybe you can learn some useful information. It will also give you something productive to do. I promised your Uncle I wouldn't let you sit around all day."

"Work at the comic store? That would be awesome!"

"That's the spirit Taz. Then the last clue we have is Project Overlord… I can't think of what that could be." Hunter put the business card for the piano bar in his pocket and opened the door. He paused, then looked back over his shoulder. "Taz, keep my knife with you at all times." He left Taz and Moja alone in the room.

Taz jumped up on the bed, kicked off his shoes, and turned on the television. He opened a big bag of potato chips, then patted the bed with his hand, signaling for Moja to come sit next to him. She wagged her tail and quickly leaped up. She sat next to him, patiently waiting for Taz to give her a potato chip.

"To think I was going to spend the summer milking the cows and cleaning up after the chickens. Things are starting to look pretty good for us, right Moja?" He handed her a chip and rubbed her head. The treat was gone in a millisecond. She licked her lips and stared at his hand, as it re-entered the bag. "I'll start calling the banks right after this cartoon finishes."

That night, Hunter drove to the piano bar. Along the way, he was deep in thought. Being alone in the car gave him a chance to think about the events leading up to this moment. His memories still hadn't returned. As he drove, he looked at all of the advertisement billboards. After a while, they all started to look the same. The colorful city lights reflected on the hood of the car. They reminded him of his dreams. He still frequently dreamt of the blue light and the two burning red eyes, but still didn't know what they meant.

He parked the car down the street from the piano bar and stepped out onto the street. After pausing for a moment, he opened the trunk and put on the black leather jacket. It fit him perfectly. As he walked away from the car, he couldn't help but look up at the gigantic skyscrapers and the streets around him. There were so many people walking in every direction. He'd never seen anything like it, at least, he thought he hadn't.

The entrance to the bar was down a narrow alleyway. The alley was gritty and covered in graffiti. Exhaust steam from buildings either side filled the narrow space. A large bouncer sat on a stool in front of the entrance. Hunter approached slowly and the bouncer held the door open for him. Directly at the entrance there were a set of dimly lit stairs leading down to the basement where the bar was located.

When Hunter reached the lower level, he looked around at the dark dingy atmosphere. Red curtains covered the walls and there were black and white tiles on the floor. It was poorly lit. In the center of the room, there was a slightly elevated stage with a black grand piano. Around the stage, were several tables, with the bar situated in the corner. He looked at the other guests. They were mostly older men, all wearing suits and smoking cigars. Hunter sat down at an empty table near the back and watched the cigar smoke slowly drift through the air.

A waitress approached his table. She wore a red corset and black leggings. As soon as he saw her, Hunter started to feel uncomfortable.

"Hello stranger, what can I get for you?" She leaned towards him in a seductive way.

"I'll take a sparkling water, thanks." Hunter smiled at her, nervously.

"Sparkling water? Is that a joke?" She asked.

"No, why would that be a joke?" A bewildered Hunter tried to understand what she meant.

"We don't serve water, we serve alcohol." The waitress replied.

"Just bring me whatever you think is best?" Hunter said, as

she rolled her eyes and left the table. Hunter watched her go to the bar and speak to the bar tender. The waitress returned with a tall, thin glass, containing a pale green liquid.

"There you go sweetheart, one Technarita, enjoy the show."

Hunter picked up the glass and stared at the drink. He took a small sip, and although it tasted like poison, he tried to look like he enjoyed the taste. As he sipped the drink, the lights went dark, and a spotlight appeared on the stage. A beautiful woman, with dark hair wearing a skin-tight red dress approached the piano. She looked incredible. She walked right past Hunters table and for a split second, the two made eye contact. She sat at the piano and started to play a slow melancholy melody.

The music captivated Hunter. Her deep voice sang soulful and mysterious lyrics. As he tried to understand the meaning of her words, someone tapped him on the shoulder. Hunter turned to look at a short fat man with a messy beard, smoking a cigar, who was sitting next to him.

"Isn't she great?" The man said.

"Yeah, she's amazing. Who is she?" Hunter replied.

"That's Nakita, the bosses girl, she plays here every night."

"The bosses girl? What does that mean?" Hunter asked, as the man took a deep smoke from his cigar.

"You know, the boss. That's his girl." The man exhaled smoke directly at Hunter. "It means hands off, or you'll leave in a body bag, hahaha!" He cackled like a demented hyena. "I haven't seen you here before. What brings you to our fabulous establishment?"

"A friend of mine recommended it." Hunter replied.

"Your friend sounds like a guy with good taste. I'm Simon, the manager, nice to meet you." Simon stuck out his fat greasy hand. As they chatted, Hunter watched Nakita. She sat perfectly still, except for her hands, as they fluttered around the white and black keys. She played for a short while, then stood up from the piano.

"So kid, do you want to meet the artist? You can talk to her, but whatever you do, don't touch her. Understand?"

"Hey Nakita, you've got a fan over here." Simon waved her over to the table and she sat next to Hunter. "I'll be back in a bit." Simon left the table and the two sat in silence. Hunter nervously smiled at her. She looked even more attractive up close. Her skin was slightly tanned and her dark hair was perfectly styled. She wore dark eyeliner and her deep blue eyes would hypnotize any man who gazed upon her.

"So uh… I really liked your song." Hunter broke the silence.

"Thank you." Nakita looked directly into his eyes.

"It was incredible." Hunter continued. Nakita was used to men giving her compliments and she'd learned from experience, that such compliments, were never sincere. "The notes that you played were so mystical. I didn't expect to hear something like that in a place like this. Is it your own song?"

"Um, yes it is." She replied. She'd never been asked that question before. "Did you really like it?" She asked softly.

"Of course, but I'm not sure I completely understood what you were singing about."

"The song's not actually finished yet. It's about the human soul. If you allow darkness inside it will consume you, but even the darkest of souls can be redeemed."

"Does the song have a name?" Hunter asked.

"Not yet, I need to finish it first, besides, I don't see much point in naming it. No one comes here to listen to my music."

"You should..." Before Hunter could finish his sentence, he was interrupted by a tall man with curly red hair and a well-trimmed ginger beard.

"Nakita, come here. The shows over." She stood up from the table without saying a word and walked towards the man who was holding a door open for her. As she walked through the doorway, she made eye contact with Hunter again. Then she was gone.

"Better luck next time, buddy." Simon laughed, as he sat back down. Hunter quickly got over the awkwardness of the situation and remembered why he had come here in the first place.

"Simon, my friend who recommended this place to me, his name is Michael Paris. I was thinking you might have seen him here before, maybe recently?" Simon looked at Hunter and paused for a moment before replying.

"Never heard of him..." He took another deep drag from his cigar.

"Alright, well thanks for introducing me to Nakita. Goodbye Simon." Hunter stood up from the table, then walked towards the stairway leading back up to entrance.

"See you around kid." Simon watched him leave and signaled to a security man standing in the corner.

Hunter stepped out into the alleyway outside. It was the middle of the night and it had started to rain. No one was around. The bouncer put his hand on Hunter's shoulder.

"Excuse me, sir, you forgot something." The bouncer said.

Hunter turned to face him. It wasn't the same bouncer from when he had arrived. The man looked familiar, dressed in a black suit. Then Hunter felt something sharp pinch his abdomen. The man thrust a knife deep into Hunter's stomach and his body went limp. He fell into the man's arms, who dragged him down the alleyway, away from the bar. He placed Hunter in the back of a neighboring building and left him to die. Hunters body slumped on the floor, as blood poured out from the knife wound. The man straightened out his suit, then walked back towards the piano bar.

As Hunter lay on the ground, the consciousness left his body. Images flashed in his mind; Black, infinite darkness. Out of the void, a ghostly image appeared. The spirit looked humanoid, but was covered in gigantic metallic armor and wielded a large sword. The figure knelt down to pick up a severed arm and held it out towards Hunter.

"This is why you're here. You must try to remember."

Hunter couldn't speak. He looked at the hand, which dripped with blood. The blood pooled on the ground and each new droplet exploded into flames, like lava from a volcano. He spoke to Hunter again.

"I've given you a gift. Now use it!"

The ghost let go of the severed hand. It fell in slow motion towards the pool of fire and blood. Upon impact, everything exploded into a thousand tiny pieces of crystal shards.

Hunters blood flowed slowly along the ground, mixing with raindrops, as they fell from the sky. The fingers on his left hand started to twitch. He opened his eyes. He could feel his body again and he felt powerful. He pulled himself up to his feet.

When he looked down at his wound, he couldn't believe what he saw. A gush of blue energy appeared to pour out from the wound and surround his body. He stared at his hands, which were now glowing in a soft, blue light. His wound quickly healed and his whole body began to vibrate. He made a fist with his left hand causing Phthalo Blue energy to surround it, like a glove. The man in the black suit turned around to look at Hunter. He couldn't believe what he was seeing.

"What the hell is going on?" That man reached into his pocket and pulled out his knife again. "Say your prayers, you freak!" He slashed at Hunter, but the Phthalo Blue energy surrounding him acted like a shield. It couldn't be penetrated. Hunter grabbed the man's wrist and squeezed until every bone had shattered. Hunter now recognized his attacker. He was the same man who killed Michael Paris at the docks. Hunter let go of his wrist and the man fell to the floor, screaming in agony. He looked up at Hunter and begged for his life. Hunter once again looked at his hands, which were now glowing even stronger. The man pleaded, but Hunter couldn't hear his words. Hunter looked directly into the man's eyes, then walked away.

3 PHTHALO BLUES

Tech City, Middle Continent
Day 8 Month 3 Year 2037

Hunter sat on the hood of the black sports car and looked up at the night sky. The stars sparkled and reflected in the rippling waters of Tech City. He parked just outside of the city limit, on the other side of South Bridge. He looked at the cityscape, as the water glowed in the near distance. It had been a month since the incident at the piano bar. The investigation into the disappearance of Max had run cold and Hunter questioned his motives.

As he lay on the hood of the car, he thought back to the artist's cabin. He would love nothing more right now, than to sit on the grass and listen to the birds, while he watched the stream flow slowly along the muddy bank. Tech City seemed like an infinite enigma, impossible to decipher. No matter how many streets he explored, or how many people he spoke to, there were still endless possibilities to the answers he was looking for. He contemplated whether he should return to Valley Village and begin his journey all over again.

He questioned what he was actually looking for and what was his purpose in life. Was he looking for his memories? Was he looking for Max? Was this really why he was meant to come to Tech City? He thought about the mysterious figure who told him to travel to Tech City in the first place. Who was he? What did he want Hunter to find? Hunter had no clue. All he did know, was that Michael Paris had been killed by a thug from the Tech City Piano Bar. Strangely, the body of Michael Paris had been discovered, but there was no formal investigation by the Tech City Police. No one seemed to care.

Hunter turned his attention away from the city and looked at his left hand, while he made a fist. As he clenched, Phthalo Blue energy would pulse from his skin, like a glove. He watched the blue light, as he made it appear and disappear. He could now partially control the energy, but still hadn't learned to harness it's power completely. He could feel it flowing through his veins, but the fact that he didn't understand why he had this gift, made him feel even more helpless.

The only things in his life which brought him joy were Taz and Moja. Both had adapted well to the lifestyle of Tech City and never seemed happier. Although he was the adult and leader of the group, he needed them much more than they needed him. Only one other thing filled him with optimism and that was the image of Nakita in his mind playing piano. No matter how hard he tried, he couldn't forget her beauty and how good she looked in that skin-tight red dress. He would often return to the alleyway outside of the Tech City Piano Bar and hide in the shadows, hoping to get a glimpse of her. After hours of contemplation, he drove back to the Dolphin Inn.

"Good morning Taz," Hunter poured himself a cup of coffee, as he looked at all of the clues from his investigation. The same clues he had been looking at for the past month.

"Hunter, I told you before, you have to wait for the right conditions for the solution to show itself. Just like my puzzle, remember? Try to find something to take your mind off the investigation, check this out." Taz sat up in his bed, then clicked his fingers. "Moja fetch." She jumped up and ran to the other side of the room, then carried Taz's slippers in her mouth back to him. "Good, now drop it and sit." Moja placed the slippers on the floor next to the bed, then sat staring up at Taz, with her mouth open and tongue slightly hanging out. "Good doggy Moja." Taz rubbed her ears.

"Taz, that's amazing! Did you teach her that yourself?" Hunter was genuinely impressed.

"Of course, what do you think I do while you're out spying on the piano bar." Taz gave Moja a treat as a reward.

"You know Taz, I'm really glad you came with me on this trip." Hunter said.

"I know what you're trying to do. Nice try, Hunter, but I'm still keeping all the money from Max's mother. You owe me for my treasure, remember?"

"Taz, you're too smart for me. Speaking of Max, let's just have a quick review. Tell me again about the comic book store." Taz answered Hunter's questions, while he brushed his teeth in the small hotel bathroom.

"The store looks totally normal. The manager Steve is a bit of a geek and doesn't have a girlfriend. Other than that, he's alright. I like working there. There doesn't seem to be anything about that place that could somehow be related to Max's disappearance." Taz's speech was muffled by the toothbrush in his mouth.

"Just in case, I'm going to come visit you again today while you're at work. What about the key?" Hunter asked. Taz leaned his head into the doorway, so he could talk directly to Hunter.

"Hunter, I tried every bank in the city, twice. I even tried all the postal services, in case it was for a post box or something. It doesn't belong to any of them. According to a locksmith, the key is for a very unusually type of lock. What about the piano bar? They must know something. If one of their employees killed Michael Paris, then they might also be somehow involved with Max."

"There's definitely something going on there, but it's too dangerous." Hunter hadn't told Taz much about what happened on the night when he first visited the piano bar. His Phthalo Blue power was still a secret.

"We'll find the answer, we just need to be patient. I'm taking Moja to the park. Then I'm working at Big World Comics in the afternoon. See you later Hunter." Taz paused, then had an idea. "Wait, do you want to come with us? It might help take your mind off the investigation."

"Actually Taz, I think I would like that." Hunter looked at Taz and grinned. "I'll just come for a short time. Do you want me to drive us?"

"Nah, the metro is much more fun. Moja loves to ride the shuttle."

Taz, Hunter, and Moja, arrived at 'Organics Park' in the center of Tech City. The park was full of tall trees and greenery, a vast contrast to the energetic city surrounding it. It was a popular location for dog owners and there were many other people out walking on this warm sunny day. Luckily, Moja had become quite tame, thanks to Taz's supervision. She didn't even acknowledge most of the other dogs, as they slowly walked through the park.

Along the way, they crossed path with a high-class lady walking with a smaller breed of dog. The little dog started growling at Moja, and Moja replied with a loud bark. She ran forward towards the little dog and sniffed its behind. Her tail wagged, as the little dog jumped around, trying to nip at Moja. She was intuitive enough to know the little dog was no real threat. She responded, by prodding the small dog with her snout.

Organics Park was a mini oasis of nature within the urban landscape of Tech City. It reminded them of Valley Village. As they continued to explore the surrounding greenery, Hunter suggested they get some food from a nearby café. When they entered, Hunter waived Moja's leash at the waitress. She replied with a nod, signaling they were allowed to bring her inside the café.

"We'd go out of business if we didn't allow dogs. What can I get for you?" The waitress asked.

"Anything but catula sprouts," Taz replied.

"I see, well how about some cherry pie?" She grinned at him.

"Yes!" Taz was very happy with her suggestion.

"This is a nice place," Hunter said, as he looked out of the window. On one side there was the park full of nature. On the other side were huge buildings and streets full of pedestrians.

They sat at the counter, chatting about everything unrelated to the investigation. They reminisced about Valley Village and spoke fondly about Sister Mary. Taz still had a crush on her. As they ate their pie, a woman with dark hair, wearing a white tank-top, casual jeans, and sunglasses, came into the café to order a coffee. The woman seemed distracted. She repeatedly looked over her shoulder, checking the entrance to the café. The waitress placed the coffee on the counter and the woman started to pour some sugar. She turned again to check behind her and accidentally knocked over the cup. Coffee spilled all over the counter and down onto Hunters lap.

"I'm so sorry!" The woman said, embarrassed. She picked up the cup and placed some napkins on the counter. Hunter stood up, then couldn't believe who he was talking to.

"Nakita?!?" He said. She paused and looked at Hunter.

"Do I know you?" She removed her sunglasses. "Oh my god! You're the guy that messed up Jake!" She fearfully stumbled back and fell to the floor.

"It's ok, I won't hurt you." He reached out his hand and looked her in the eyes. She stared back, and after a short pause, slowly took his hand. He helped her to her feet. "I think you dropped these." Hunter picked up her sunglasses.

"Thanks…Sorry about the coffee." She nervously smiled at him.

"Aren't you going to introduce me?" Taz stood up from the counter. "I'm Taz, nice to meet you." He had a big grin on his face. Nakita awkwardly waved at him. "Unfortunately, I'm late for work, so I'll leave the two of you alone." Taz winked at Hunter, then took Moja by the leash. He leaned over to Hunter and whispered. "You owe me another one for this." Hunter raised his eyebrow and watched Taz leave the cafe.

"Would you like another coffee?" Hunter said, as he turned to face Nakita.

"Um sure, yeah, why not." She was clearly nervous about talking to him. After checking the entrance again, she put her sunglasses back on and sipped her coffee.

"Did you ever finish your song?" Hunter asked.

"My song? Oh, not yet, I've been busy." She replied.

"Is everything alright? I've noticed you keep checking over your shoulder. Is someone following you?"

"No, it's just a force of habit. Can we sit down?" She pointed to an empty table.

"Of course." Hunter wasn't sure why she seemed so anxious.

"Why did you do that to Jake?" She asked cautiously.

"Jake? You mean the bouncer outside? I was just defending myself. Nakita, how much do you know about the piano bar?"

"Well, the owner is Alex, he's my boyfriend. He would kill me if he knew I was talking to you. Are you a member of a rival gang or something?"

"Rival gang? No, I'm sort of like a private investigator. I'm looking for a missing child."

"Another missing child?" She couldn't hide the shock on her face.

"What do you mean another one?" Hunter felt he was onto something.

"I'm not sure. I shouldn't be talking about this. Alex is crazy about stuff like that. I've overheard a few people at the bar talking about missing children. It's related to something called Project Overlord. Alex has been talking about it for the past six months."

"Project Overlord…Nakita, please tell me everything you know. It's incredibly important." This line of questioning, seemed to make her even more agitated.

"I don't know anything else. Listen, you seem like a nice guy, so I'll tell you now. Ever since that night, Alex and the guys have been talking about you. Don't come back to the piano bar, or they'll kill you this time for sure. I have to go."

"Nakita wait!" He tried to stop her, but she ran from the café and disappeared into the crowd of pedestrians.

Taz arrived at Big World Comics and hung his leather rucksack on the coat rack. He sat behind the counter and checked everything was where it should be.

"Hey Steve, sorry I'm late." Taz placed a baseball cap on his head bearing the logo 'B.W.C'. It was a relatively large store, located down a small street, but always had customers. He flicked through some newly delivered comics and watched cartoons on a tiny television positioned behind the counter. Although it didn't pay much, it was an easy job and Taz loved it.

Later that day, while the store was empty, Taz got up to stretch his legs. He walked outside and leaned against the wall next to the entrance of the store. He looked up at the clear blue sky and thought about the last month living in Tech City. As far as Taz was concerned, he wanted to stay here forever. The city had so much energy and he made friends quickly with the kids who visited the store. Although he was fond of Valley Village and his Uncle, he always dreamt of leaving someday. He thought about how he must be the coolest kid ever to be living in Tech City. The other orphans and more importantly, Sister Mary, would never believe that he had a job in the biggest city on Middle Continent. He took off his cap and looked at the logo for the comic store. Then he saw someone approaching in the corner of his eye.

"I was wondering what time you'd show up. Did you have a nice date?" Taz asked.

"It wasn't a date. She's just someone I met at the piano bar. I'm going to take look around." Hunter entered the store and started looking at the different comics on the shelves. He saw a bin full of various posters. One, in particular, caught his eye.

"Taz, come check this out. This is the blueprints for the construction plans of Tech City, pretty cool isn't it."

"Hahaha, Hunter you're a genius."

"What do you mean?" Hunter didn't understand.

"You don't see it? Like I said, you have to wait for the right conditions in order for the solution to present itself. Look at the numbers up the side of the poster."

"Wait a second...They're the same as the keyring! The numbers must be coordinates on this map! I've got to go back to the hotel to get the key. I can't believe we didn't figure this out sooner." As Hunter took the poster and went to leave the store.

"Um Hunter, aren't you forgetting something? It's twenty woolongs for the poster." Taz said.

"Right, sorry, here you go Taz. I'll let you know what I find." Hunter handed him the money

"Ok, keep me posted. You're welcome by the way." Taz watched Hunter, as he hastily left the store. He took off his cap again and brushed his hand through his hair. He grinned arrogantly, as he thought about how awesome he was. He picked up a comic off the shelf and walked back behind the counter.

Back at the Dolphin Inn, Hunter looked at the keyring and laughed to himself. The numbers pointed to a location on the map that wasn't far from the hotel and not very far from where

Michael Paris had been murdered. He drove to the area, which was an empty construction plot, next to a large factory. After walking to the exact location, he looked at the ground and started digging with his hands. There had to be something there.

He looked around to see if anyone else was nearby, then felt something solid in the dirt. He tried to remove it, but it was stuck firmly in the ground. He brushed away the earth to reveal a metallic object with a lock, almost like a safe, built into the ground. As he inserted the key, he felt the anticipation of finally discovering a new clue to his investigation. When the key turned, the front face of the metallic object lifted open. The contents had been vacuum sealed. When the seal was broken, steam blew out and revealed a small cavity. Inside was a folder, which was labeled:

PROJECT OVERLORD - CLASSIFIED UNDER ORDERS OF PRESIDENT CHAKOTAY OF CAPITOL CITY

He took the file back to the car and sat in the driver's seat, reading the documents in the folder. One by one, he placed them on the dashboard. He was dumbfounded by what he was discovering. With each new piece of information, his outrage grew stronger. When he had finished reading every document, he placed them all back in the folder and laid it on the passenger seat. He was in complete shock. He hung his head on the steering wheel and clenched his fists in anger. Phthalo Blue energy pulsated around him. After a short moment, he reached into his pocket and pulled out a mobile telephone. He dialed the only number saved in the phone's history and tried to speak calmly.

"Katrin, It's me, I know what happened to your son. He was kidnapped by a gang who operate secretly out of the Tech City Piano Bar. They have taken many children over the past six months. All of the others were homeless war orphans living on the streets. Your son was taken by mistake. They probably mistook him as an orphan, while he was walking home from the comic book store. I don't know what has happened to these children, but I'm going to find out. This whole thing is very well organized. It's called Project Overlord. Michael Paris was hired directly by the President of Capitol City, to investigate all the reports of missing children in Tech City. You need to call the police and tell them everything. I'll come to your apartment very soon to give you all the evidence I have collected. You should give it to the police. Then I'm going to the piano bar to get your son back."

Hunter drove towards the Katrin Fielder's apartment building. Along the way the way he called the comic book store and explained everything to Taz.

"Taz listen, this is a dangerous situation. If I'm not back by tomorrow, take all of the money and buy a bus ticket back to Berlin. Don't tell anyone where you are going and don't say goodbye to any of your friends. Just take Moja and get out of the city as quickly as you can. From Berlin, take the first boat back to Lyme Cove."

"Hunter, if this is so dangerous, why not let the police handle it?" Taz asked.

"Because now I know for certain, this is why we were meant to come to Tech City. This is what the man in black wanted us to find. I'll be alright Taz. There's something that I've been keeping secret from you for some time now. I don't know how to explain it, but trust me, I'm not in any danger. If anyone should be scared, it's them."

Hunter pulled up to the apartment building, but something was wrong. There was a police car parked outside and the entrance to the building had been forced open. Hunter ran inside, then took the elevator up to the thirtieth floor. As the elevator moved up the building, Hunter began clenching his fists. As the elevator doors opened, he was shocked to see Katrin Fielder lying dead on the carpet. There was a police officer standing over her body.

"What happened?" Yelled Hunter. The officer looked at him, but didn't reply.

"He's here," the officer spoke into his radio. Hunter was confused as to what was going on. Then Jake stepped out of Katrin's apartment, with a cast on his arm and another officer at his side.

"What is going on here?!? Officers, this man is a murderer, arrest him." Hunter pointed at Jake.

"You fool, don't you know? We own the police." Jake pulled a silver baton from his pocket and started walking towards Hunter. "Guys, keep your guns pointed at him at all times. He's a tricky one. I just want you to know, we wouldn't have had to kill her if you hadn't been looking where you weren't supposed to be. We thought when we killed Mr. Paris that would be the end of it, but then you showed up. You're a hard man to track down. But like a moth to a flame, you've come to us. We've had her phone tapped ever since we discovered we accidentally took her kid." Jake pushed a button on the baton, which made it electrify. "I brought this just in case you try any of your tricks. I'm going to enjoy making you suffer, you freak!"

Hunter looked at Jake and the police officers who were now pointing their guns directly at him.

"What have you done with Max, and the other children?" Hunter spoke with authority.

"You're never going to find out." Jake said, as he raised the baton above his head, preparing to strike. Hunter looked Jake in the eyes and exploded with rage as Phthalo Blue energy engulfed his body. "Die, freak!" Jake swung the baton as hard as he could, but before it made contact, Hunter grabbed Jake's wrist with one hand. He put his other hand around Jakes' neck and lifted him off the ground by the throat. Hunter looked him in the eyes as he squeezed tightly, choking him to death.

"You'll never hurt another child ever again, Jake!" Bullets from the officers ricocheted around Hunter. Jake couldn't breathe. He tried to get the officers to help, but their bullets couldn't penetrate the Phthalo Blue energy barrier, which protected Hunter. As a final effort, Jake thrust his electronic baton into Hunter's face. For a brief moment, Hunter was stunned. Unfortunately for Jake, Hunter soon regained control, and continued to squeeze Jakes throat harder, and harder, until the life left his body. When Jake was dead, Hunter let go and watched his body fall to the floor. He couldn't believe he had just killed a man. Hunter turned to the police officers, who were terrified.

"I don't want to kill you, but I will if you don't put an end to Project Overlord. This has to stop." Blue energy pulsated from his body, as the officers ran away as quickly as they could. Hunter left the apartment building and headed straight to confront Alex at the piano bar.

Hunter drove straight down the alley and stopped right in front of the bar. At the entrance, a different bouncer sat on a stool smoking a cigarette.

"Hey pal, you can't leave your car there. You'll need to park it on the street around the corner."

"I don't have time for that, let me in," Hunter stepped out from the car.

"Wow kid, you're really desperate to get some action tonight. Seriously, move the damn car!"

"I have a better idea." Hunter walked up to the bouncer who took a defensive stance. He tried to punch Hunter, but ended up with his fist clamped in Hunter's grip. He cried out in pain as his hand broke. Then Hunter pushed him to the side.

Hunter walked down the stairs, then entered the bar. Nakita was playing piano and the bar almost full.

"You must have a death wish to come back here," Simon signaled to the back. "Why don't you make this easy, we don't want to make a scene in front of our guests." He grinned nervously.

"Get out of my way you fat piece of shit." Hunter shoved him back and walked across the bar. He engaged any bouncer that got in his way. Several converged on his position and everyone in the lounge watched the situation unfold. Nakita stopped playing. She sat at the piano and watched Hunter incapacitate each bouncer. When there was no one left to fight him, he went back and grabbed Simon. Hunter dragged him across the bar, then slammed him onto a table.

"Take me to your boss, now!" Hunter aggressively asked.

"I can't, he's not here." Simon was panting and scared for his life.

"I'm not leaving until I see him, I'll break every bone in your body!" Hunter leaned on him hard. Simon cried out in pain, then Hunter released his grip and turned to face Nakita. Simon crawled under the table, cowering in fear. "Nakita, where's Alex?!"

"Right here!" A door behind one of the curtains flew open and Alex stepped out with several armed guards. Alex stood dressed in an expensive suit. His curly red hair was tied back in a ponytail. "Before you get any crazier, why don't we talk about this calmly upstairs, I'll tell you everything you want to know." Hunter looked at him. After a short pause, he nodded. "Good, we're making progress. Simon, come out from under there. Why do you have to be such a pussy? Nakita, you come as well, I want you to hear this. Everyone else, get back to work." The guards escorted Hunter through to the back.

"Everything you need to know is up here." Alex pushed a button for the elevator. When the doors opened, the interior was covered in gold and marble. "You know, we've been looking for you for some time. I have every resource at my disposal and we couldn't even find out your name. Just to satisfy my curiosity, who are you?"

"My name is...Hunter."

"Well Hunter, I'm Alex, nice to meet you." He smiled as he tried to engage Hunter in small talk during the long elevator ride to the top of the building. "Too bad about Jake, he was a good worker. I guess I'll be looking for a replacement." When the doors opened, Hunter was surprised to see they were on top of a very large skyscraper. They stepped out and assembled on the rooftop.

"Look at that view. Tech City, isn't it magnificent?"

"I didn't come here to look at the city, where are the children Alex?" Hunter stared directly at him.

"Patience, Hunter. You have some very impressive abilities. My men didn't stand a chance against you. Poor Jake. But do you know what the most powerful weapon of all is? Fear. You see all these people? They do what I tell them, not because I pay them, but because they fear me. Simon fears me and Nakita fears me, don't you darling? Nakita tells me everything. Just like she told me about your little meeting at the café. She told me, because she knows if she kept any secrets from me, I'd kill her.

That's the power of fear and before the end of this night, Hunter, you will fear me as well."

The night sky was silent, except for the sound of Alex's voice, as he gave his speech. A small breeze agitated the air high up on top of the building.

"So you want to know about the children? First, why don't I introduce our other guest." Alex clicked his fingers. One of his guards came to the roof, dragging Taz, who was bound and tied. "Don't get any ideas, Hunter. I wouldn't want to have to kill him. I would rather use him for the project. He looks about the right age. He'll be a valuable specimen. Can you believe he came right to us? I get a phone call from one of my men, saying some kid is trying to sneak into the bar. Nakita told us you had a little friend. It wasn't hard to figure out he was with you." Hunter looked at Taz, and then back at Alex, and Nakita. He was very nervous about the situation. Alex smiled as he knew he was in control. "Now you're going to do exactly what I tell you, or my men will throw the little guy off the roof." Alex walked over to Taz and roughly grabbed him by his hair. "Are you scared, kid? I think you fear me already, don't you?"

"Alex, he's just a boy," Nakita pleaded.

"Shut up, bitch!" Alex walked back over to her side and looked at Hunter. "Simon told me how you like to watch her playing the piano. Pathetic, do you really think she would ever be interested in you, you're nobody. I'm the most powerful man in Tech City. I own the cops. I own the streets. I can have anything, or anyone I want. *I am* the Overlord!" Hunter looked at him and then spoke calmly and confidently.

"You might be the overlord, but I am the Hunter and you are my prey." Hunter closed his eyes and gripped his fists. Blue energy shot out towards the guard holding Taz, like a bolt of lightning. The energy engulfed the man, who fell to the ground writhing in pain.

"Taz run!" Hunter yelled, then he proceeded to eliminate the armed guards. For some, he used his fists to smash their bodies, for the others, he used lightning bolts of energy. He quickly decimated Alex's forces and left bodies scattered across the roof of the skyscraper. All that remained standing were Alex, Nakita, Simon, and Taz, who hid behind Hunter.

"Hunter, help me get these things off!" Taz untied the ropes which bound his arms. "You're not so tough anymore are you?!" He started kicking the guard who had been holding him.

"Taz, hold on, we need to finish this." Hunter walked over to Alex and Nakita.

"That...that's not possible?!?!?" Alex stood in shock, looking at the bodies of his men. "You're not human. You can't be."

"It doesn't matter what I am, where are the children?" Hunter firmly grabbed Alex by his suit. Alex said nothing. "Start talking or I'll throw *you* off the roof!"

"They're gone. Listen, this wasn't my idea. I'm just a guy they hired. They said they needed children for some experiment. It's called Project Overlord. I just did what they told me to."

"Who told you?" Hunter tightened his grip.

"The Government! Some politician in Capitol City hired us." Alex squirmed.

"Was it the President?" Hunter was trying to understand the situation.

"No way, it was someone else. They paid us a lot of money. He's from a group. They call themselves 'Nexus'. He said it was top secret. I promise, I don't know what happened to the children."

"Where are they now?" He looked at Alex, who trembled in fear.

"I don't know. We packed them in the back of lorries and sent them over North Bridge. We met their contact out in the desert. They took the shipment somewhere else. I'm guessing it was back to Capitol City. That's all I know, I swear."

Nakita watched Alex and an expression of remorse, and sadness, came over her face.

"Look, I was just following orders. I didn't do anything wrong. Killing me won't bring them back or change anything. If you want to find them, you'll need me. I'll do anything you want, please!" Alex begged.

"When is the next shipment?" Hunter was trying to devise a plan.

"In two days. Hunter, listen, I can help you! You'll need me to get them back!"

"How many children have you taken so far?"

"…About fifty." Hunter let go of Alex. He looked at Taz, who had a cut above his eye.

"Taz, let's go. We're going to Capitol City to find Max and the others." Hunter walked away from Alex towards Taz.

"Hunter Wait!" Nakita cried out. She ran over to them. "I didn't know what he was doing. I didn't know about any of this." Hunter looked at her. He wasn't sure if she could be trusted.

"How dare you bitch, I own you!" Alex pulled out a gun and pointed it at Nakita. Hunter quickly shot a bolt of energy towards Alex. It exploded and the impact drove him back towards the edge of the roof. An image of Max' picture flashed in Hunter's mind. Hunter narrowed his eyes, then with a slight thrust of his fist, the energy pushed Alex over the edge. Alex screamed, as he fell from the skyscraper all the way to the streets below.

"Simon, tell all of Alex's men that their reign of terror is over. If any other child goes missing, I'll come back and kill every last one of them. I'll kill you too Simon."

"Yes, yes whatever you say." Simon was completely paralyzed with fear.

"Taz, are you Ok?" Hunter put his arm around Taz.

"Yeah, I'm fine. Hunter that was amazing. How did you do that?" Taz was fascinated by the blue energy which surrounded Hunter.

"I'll explain everything back at the hotel. Let's get out of here. Nakita, if you want, you can come with us." Hunter, Taz, and Nakita left, as Simon stood on top of the building, looking at the bodies around him.

"After I left the comic book store, I was headed back to the hotel, but…I wanted to help you. So I came here instead. When I arrived, some guy grabbed me. I wanted to use your knife, but I left it in the hotel room. Moja's still there, I hope she's ok. I'm sorry Hunter." Taz explained his story, as they approached the car.

Hunter thought about what Taz had said. He wanted to tell him how careless and naïve he was. He wanted to tell him how he could have gotten himself killed. But really, he was just happy

Taz was safe.

"We're all ok, that's what's important. Taz, you should have listened to me." He paused for a moment, noticing the tears in Taz' eyes. "Let's get back to the Dolphin Inn and check on Moja. Then we can figure out what to do next."

Before she entered the black sports car, Nakita had something she needed to say.

"Taz, I'm sorry. I told Alex who you were after we met at the café. I didn't know he would do this to you. I've seen him do terrible things, but never to children." She spoke with a somber voice.

Hunter drove through the streets of Tech City. Nakita sat in the front passenger seat, with Taz in the back. The three sat in silence, looking out at the city nightlife, as it passed by. Hunter looked at Taz in the rearview mirror, then glanced at Nakita. She looked back at him and smiled. She was wearing her red dress, with a small jacket. Nakita was unsure about what would come next for her, but whatever happened, she was happy to be away from Alex and his gang.

Back at the Dolphin Inn, Hunter opened the door to their room and Moja ran out to greet them. She wagged her tail and jumped up with her paws on Taz, then started licking his face.

"Moja stop it!" Taz tried to push her away. Then she did the same to Hunter.

"Oh, that's right. I remember from the café, you have a dog…" Nakita looked uncomfortable.

"Don't worry, she's friendly, she won't bite." Hunter tried to reassure her.

"If you say so." Nakita stared uncomfortably at Moja.

"You're not scared are you?" Taz grinned.

"No, I just didn't think you guys would have a dog with a pink sparkly collar."

"I told you," Taz said to Hunter.

"Ok, let's sit down quickly and figure out what happens next." Hunter offered Nakita a chair. When she sat down, Moja shoved her head on Nakita's lap and started sniffing her.

"Oh ugh, down girl, good doggy, please stay down." Nakita squirmed in her chair, trying to get Moja to leave her alone.

"She's just excited to meet someone new." Taz chuckled. He pulled her away from Nakita. "Hunter what the hell was that blue light coming from your body. Are you like a superhero or something?"

"I don't know what it is. It started the first night I went to the piano lounge. I got stabbed and thought I was going to die. Then this blue light started pouring out from my body. I don't know what it is, but it's incredibly powerful."

"This is so awesome," Taz petted Moja, who had calmed down and lay under the table.

"Hunter, are you really going to Capitol City?" Nakita asked softly.

"I guess so. We came here looking for something. I believe we've found what we're looking for. Now it's time to leave."

"Did you come here looking for the missing children?" Nakita asked.

"Not exactly, it's a long story." Hunter replied.

"If you're going, then I would like to come with you. I want to help find those children. I never knew Alex could have been so evil. There's nothing for me here. I just want to leave."

"Are you sure? This is going to be a long journey and it's going to be dangerous." Hunter said.

"I'm absolutely certain." Although she wished her words were genuine. Secretly, she was deeply conflicted.

"I guess I'll call Steve and tell him I'm not coming into to work tomorrow. I'm going to miss Tech City." Taz sighed.

"Taz…never mind. Let's get some sleep. Nakita, you can stay here at the hotel, they have plenty of rooms available. We'll head out in the morning towards Berlin."

"Berlin? But Capitol City is to the north?" Nakita asked.

"I know, I just want to take a day to recover and rest. I think it would be best to do that away from Tech City. Taz and I have been there before, it's a nice town. With the car, we'll be there in a few hours. Nakita, do you need to say goodbye to anybody or tell any family where you are going?"

"I have no family…" Taz looked at her and thought about his Uncle. "Goodnight, I'll see you tomorrow."

That night, before going to bed, Hunter took a shower. He stood as the hot water cleaned the blood and dirt away from his fists. His body was aching. He looked at himself in the mirror, as the steam from the hot water clouded his view. His mind started to talk to himself.

"Am I really supposed to go to Capitol City? What is Project Overlord?

What is Nexus? What does it all mean? Every answer leads to new questions. Who am I? Will I ever find my memories?"

The next morning, Hunter got up early and made some coffee. He looked at the clues from his investigation laying on the table and placed them inside the 'Project Overlord' file. As he opened his bag to place the file inside something fell out. It was the piece of metal, which Taz had given him back in the artist's cabin. The gift from his Uncle. He held the circular piece of metal for a second and placed it back inside the bag, along with the 'Project Overlord' file. He looked at Taz snoring and then signaled to Moja. He attached her leash, then left the room to take her on a walk. As he went past Nakita's room, he saw the door was wide open and the room was empty. She'd gone. He wasn't completely surprised. He thought she probably wasn't genuine about what she had said the night before. He walked Moja along the water, to the docks where his investigation had begun, one month earlier. He looked at Tech City in the morning sunlight and said goodbye.

Back at the hotel, Taz and Hunter loaded the car with their bags.

"Can't believe you boys are finally leaving us. Here's your deposit back." The receptionist from the Dolphin Inn handed Hunter fifteen woolongs. "I had to deduct ten woolongs as a cleaning fee."

"Thanks…" Hunter put the cash in his pocket, then returned to loading their luggage into the car.

"Wait for me!" Nakita shouted, as she ran towards the car.

"I thought you'd left," Hunter was pleasantly surprised.

"I just went back to my apartment to get some things. I couldn't travel in just my dress." Hunter rolled his eyes, as she wore a black miniskirt, boots, and a small black jacket over a white tank top. She carried a small bag and a book in her hand.

"Damn, I guess this means I'm sitting in the back seat with Moja." Taz sighed.

"It's alright, I'll sit in the back. I need to get over my fear of dogs." Nakita said.

"Cool, thanks Nakita, I've got some comic books I took from the store if you wanna read something."

Hunter, Taz, Nakita, and Moja, sat in the car. They drove across South Bridge, out of Tech City, towards Berlin.

4 BERLIN BLUES

Berlin, Middle Continent
Day 10 Month 3 Year 2037

The road to Berlin from Tech City was mostly empty. Hunter drove steadily, trying to hide the fact that his body was aching from exerting so much energy the night before. As he sat in the driver's seat, he took deep breaths and tried to focus on the road ahead. The sky was overcast and there was a feeling of ambiguity in the air. The landscape was mostly flat, grassy areas, with shallow slopes. In the horizon, you could see the faint outline of the ocean far in the distance.

"Nakita, did you make friends with Moja yet?" Taz looked at her in the rearview mirror.

"I think so…she's quite feminine actually. Compared to other dogs I've seen." Moja lay on the back seat with her head resting on her front paws. In the car she could never fully relax enough to sleep and always had her eyes wide open. Every once in a while, Nakita would nervously stroke her head. Hunter would occasionally glance in the mirror to watch how Nakita acted sitting next to Moja.

"You didn't have pets growing up?" Taz asked.

"No. Well actually, I remember there were a lot of stray cats in one of the places we used to live. Sometimes we would leave our back door open so they could come into our house. But I never had a dog."

"Where was that?"

"Kunsthof, but we moved around a lot when I was young. I never really had a place I would call home. It was always changing." She looked out of the window at the moving scenery.

"What happened to your parents?"

"I'd rather not talk about it...so you guys have stayed in Berlin before?"

"Yeah, it's a pretty sleepy place. We spent a few nights there before coming to Tech City." Taz leaned back in his seat. "It's a small town. Doesn't seem like much ever really happens there. We met a jeweler who was pretty cool and stayed in the local tavern. Hunter, are we going to stay there again?" Hunter was silent, staring at the road. "Hunter?!"

"Sorry Taz, I was distracted. Yes, if they have space. It's small but cozy. Is that ok with you Nakita?" Hunter asked.

"Yeah, that's fine. Hunter, I took some money from Alex's safe before I left. The piano bar was swarming with cops, but I managed to sneak in. I can help pay our expenses on the way to Capitol City." A big smile came over Taz's face.

"That's kind of you, but we actually have plenty of money."

"That's my money." Taz insisted. Hunter looked briefly at Taz and grinned.

"Let's just get to Berlin and then we can plan everything

out." They drove in the black sports car formerly owned by detective Michael Paris. A few hours later, they arrived at the port town of Berlin.

When they entered the town they had to park the car slightly out from the center. The streets were very narrow and not really designed for cars. Berlin is located on the southern coast of Middle Continent. It's a small town, most known for its port. The buildings are old, country-style structures, and the port is full of rusty constructions. The only ships docked are small wooden fishing boats and medium-sized transport vessels. The town survived from fishing and a small amount of tourism. Seagulls calmly flew around the port, as fishermen unloaded their catch of the day. A large tavern in the town center served as a meeting point for the locals. Hunter, Taz, Nakita, and Moja walked through the town and entered the tavern, which was mostly empty.

"Hi, nice to see you again? Do you have any rooms available for tonight?" Hunter asked.

"I remember you from some weeks ago, how was Tech City?" The owner of the tavern was a middle-aged woman, who also acted as both waitress and cook. She looked at Nakita's miniskirt and raised an eyebrow.

"It was…interesting," Hunter replied.

"Good, well just like the last time you were here, we have plenty of rooms available. Did you want single or double rooms?" Taz looked at Nakita and Hunter with a smirk on his face.

"We'll take three single rooms, thank you." Hunter turned to face his friends. "Listen, I think I need to get some rest." He knelt down and kissed Moja on the snout, then went up to his room and passed out on the bed. Nakita and Taz decided to eat some lunch. They sat at a wooden table in the tavern, while Moja lay in front of the open fireplace.

"I see your dog got a new collar. She looks fancy. On the menu today is fish stew, fresh from the ocean." The hostess placed two bowls on the table. She looked at Nakita, who had removed her jacket, exposing a tattoo on her shoulder. The woman raised her eyebrow again. "...And this is for you." She placed a third bowl on the floor next to Moja, who immediately jumped up and started eating the scraps of fish. Nakita looked down at her bowl and grinned at Taz. He was equally unimpressed with the dish.

"I hate fish." He said, as he stirred the bowl with his spoon.

"Yeah...I guess it smells ok." Nakita took a small amount of stew and tasted it. "Taz, how do you know Hunter?"

"We're from Valley Village, I'm his best friend." Taz took his first taste of the fish. To his surprise, it was pretty good.

"Valley Village, I've never heard of it. Is it on Middle Continent?" She took another spoonful of the dish, which she was beginning to enjoy.

"Yeah, it's on the western side. Hunter's not actually from there. Neither am I actually, I'm from Tiberia. We found him washed up on the shores, close to the village, about a year ago. He was in pretty bad shape. We managed to heal his injuries, but he lost all of his memories."

"He lost his memories?"

"Yeah, he couldn't remember who he was or where he came from. He still can't. He spent some time in the village trying to remember. Then we started this journey together."

After finishing her meal, Moja returned to the warm flames of the fire and rolled on her back with her legs in the air. Now she could sleep peacefully, as the fire kept her warm. Taz and Nakita slowly ate their stew and got to know each other. Nakita was trying her best to seem genuine and forget her previous life in Tech City. Taz was trying his best to impress her.

"So yeah I have a girlfriend back in Valley Village. She's called Mary." Taz flicked his hair back.

"Wow Taz, that sounds nice."

"Yeah, and if I were you, I wouldn't waste your time with Hunter. He knows nothing about women."

"I'll keep that in mind," she smiled briefly.

"I mean he's a nice guy, but sometimes he's so weird. Nakita, what's that book? I noticed you've been holding it since we left Tech City."

"It's from my father…it's a journal he used to keep about his research." She was reluctant to talk about her family. But she felt she could open up, just a little.

"What happened to him?" Taz asked.

"Well, my father was a scientist. He would travel all over the world and was hardly ever home. Then one time he just never came back. For a while, it was just me and my mom, but then when I was a teenager, she got sick. Then I ended up in Tech City…"

"Sounds sad," Taz could relate. He lost his own parents at a very young age. He couldn't really remember them that much and subconsciously learned to cover up their memories. "So you never found out what happened to your father?"

"No, all I have to remember him is this book. For some reason, I held onto it all these years." She focused on the brown leather cover of the book, while she spoke.

"Can I see it?" Taz held out his hand.

"Um yes, here you go. It's mostly just random notes." She handed him the book and he flicked through some of the pages. After a few moments, he stopped on one page, which caught his eye.

"This is very interesting," Taz said slowly. "Do you mind if I keep this for a while? I would like to read it."

"Sure, go right ahead. Taz, can I take Moja on a walk? I want to get some fresh air and clear my head." Nakita left Taz sitting at the table reading the journal.

She walked outside through the narrow stone streets in the cool fresh sea air. She started to feel comfortable with Moja and walked towards the seafront. Moja didn't bark at the seagulls or boats. She had become very tame. They walked out onto a small wooden dock. Nakita and Moja stood together and looked out at the ocean. From where they were standing, they were facing south towards Southern Continent. The sun was beginning to set and the red flames reflected in the water. Moja sat on the dock looking at the horizon and let out a long soft howl. The sea breeze blew Nakitas long dark hair across her face. She thought about her life and what had happened in Tech City.

More than anything she felt guilty. Guilty for what Alex had done and guilty for the way she had lived her life in recent years. She wanted more than anything to redeem herself. She thought about Hunter losing his memories and how nice it would be if she could lose hers. Then something interrupted her moment of clarity.

"Nice view, isn't it? What brings a gorgeous girl like you to Berlin?" Nakita turned to look at the man who was talking to her.

"Uh…I'm just visiting for a few days." She smiled, politely.

"Hey sorry, I don't mean to come on so strong. It's just not every day I see someone so beautiful in town. I'm Dante. I own the jewelry shop down that street. Nice to meet you." He stuck out his hand. Dante was in his late thirties and was a successful businessman within Berlin. A big fish in a small pond. He wore a tight-fitting suit and had very neatly kept facial hair. Nakita slowly extended her hand.

"Hi Dante, I'm Nakita." She didn't really want to talk to anybody, but also didn't want to be rude.

"So what do you think of our little town, Nakita?" He turned to look out over the ocean and tried discretely to look down at her legs and body. She knew he was checking her out.

"It's a nice town. Very peaceful." She said softly.

"Yep, it's peaceful alright, considering we're as close to Southern Continent as you can safely get."

"Southern Continent? Isn't it forbidden to travel there?"

"That's basically true. No one who ever crossed the ocean to Southern Continent returned safely. Apparently it's a desolate wasteland. Nothing lives there. It's completely irradiated."

"What happened?" Nakita looked south across the water.

"You hear a lot of theories from the science community. Some religious fanatics even say humans used to live on Southern Continent many years ago. But an 'Alien from the sky' came and destroyed everything as punishment for our sins. In the dead of night you can still hear the screams from across the ocean."

"Really?" She looked at him with a sense of disbelief.

"That's what I've heard, but who knows? Maybe it's true, but one thing is certain, no one who travels to Southern Continent ever returns. That is, except for the government. They've been sending expeditions down there for some years. They fly airships back and forth quite frequently. Look, here comes one now."

A huge airship far up in the sky flew over the town. A slight rumble echoed through the air, as it flew off into the distance. Nakita and Dante looked up while Moja started growling at the foreign noise.

"I wonder what they're up to? Nakita, if you don't have any other plans, would you join me for dinner tonight?" He tried to sound as charming as possible.

"I'll think about it. Dante, it was nice meeting you." Dante couldn't help but stare at her as she walked away. He smiled and shook his head.

Back at the tavern, Taz burst into Hunter's room.

"Hunter, wake up!"

"Taz...what's going on?" Hunter tried to focus.

"Look at this book. It's from Nakita's Dad. Are you alright?" Taz noticed how tired he looked.

"Yeah, I'm fine. I was just having a really strange dream. What about the book?"

"It has the same symbols that are on the piece of metal my Uncle gave you. Just like the ones we saw in the temple. Her dad was a scientist and his book is full of them. I haven't finished reading it yet, but from what I can tell, it's some sort of ancient language. I've been trying to translate the symbols."

"Really? What do they say?" Hunter spoke with a groggy voice.

"Ok, I'm not completely certain, but the metal disc says:

'KEY TO THE HEAVENS'

The symbols we saw in the temple are a bit longer. I think they say:

'HERE LIES THE BLUE CRYSTAL SHARD
THE LAST REMAINING HOPE
HERE IT MUST REMAIN UNTIL THE RETURN
PROTECTED BY THE SHROUD OF ILLUSION
BELOW THE SURFACE, EDGE AWAITS'

It's a freaky coincidence right?"

"That is strange, but I don't see how this affects the current mission?" Hunter didn't know what to make of this new piece of information.

"I suppose it doesn't, but what are the odds? I'm going to keep reading. This is going to be useful somehow, I'm sure of it." Said Taz.

"Taz, I'm sorry, I think my body needs some more time to recover from last night."

"No worries Hunter...I'll be down in the tavern." Taz was a little disappointed at Hunter's lack of enthusiasm. As he left the room, Hunter tried to make amends.

"Taz...nicely done." The dejected Taz looked back at Hunter and smiled, before closing the door.

Downstairs, Taz sat in the tavern with a glass of milk reading the book. At that moment, Nakita returned with Moja. The sight of Taz made Moja begin to wag her tail.

"How was the walk?" Taz asked.

"Good thanks. This town is very pretty. How's the book?"

"Nakita, I'm not exactly sure how, but I think this book will be of great importance to our journey."

"What makes you say that?" Nakita watched Taz take a sip from his milk.

"I'm going to tell you a story Nakita, but first, would you like a glass of milk? It's delicious." Nakita laughed out loud. "What's up?" Taz didn't see what was so funny.

"It's nothing, I'd love one, thanks Taz." Nakita was used to men buying her drinks all the time, but never a glass of milk. She removed Moja's leash and sat at the table.

"Great, my story is a little bit long. It all started after me and Hunter decided to climb this mountain..."

~

Flashback: The Temple
Day 17 Month 1 Year 2037

On the western edge of Middle Continent was an island far away from human population. The island was lush with healthy green grass and small trees were scattered amongst the fields. On the edge were cliffs, which bore the impact of the wild aggressive ocean waves. A few miles along the coast, a small boat was tethered to an old wooden dock, which had been standing there for many years. The sea was slightly calmer in this area. It was the only way to access this hidden piece of land.

Hunter and Taz walked up the cliff away from the dock with Moja leading the way without a leash. She limped slightly with every step. When they reached the top, they could see the surrounding landscape clearly. Hunter pulled out Taz's Uncle's compass to check they were still going in the right direction.

"Can I ask you something? How did you know you would need my Uncles compass when we climbed the mountain? Taz asked.

"I saw it in my dream." Hunter replied.

Moja ran on ahead through the fields of long grass and Taz was concerned they might lose sight of her. She limped from her injured paw, but could still run much faster than Hunter or Taz. They proceeded to walk across the field, until they reached a withered old tree next to a large formation of rocks near the cliff's edge. A black crow was perched on a branch watching over them.

"I think this is it," Hunter looked around in every direction. The wind was blowing gently and the sun was beginning to set.

"How can you be sure?" Taz asked, as he took a big gulp from his water bottle. Moja sniffed the trunk of the tree and marked the soil around it. The black crow cawed, which startled her. She slowly walked away from the tree, growling at the crow, who looked directly at her.

"This is the tree I saw in my dream." Hunter walked over to examine the large jagged rocks. Then something caught his eye. A blue sparkle within one of the cracks signaled this was the right way. He searched between the rocks until he could see a slight opening. "*We could fit through here.*" He thought to himself.

"Taz, come over here and look at this!" Taz walked over to Hunter and peered inside the dark tunnel. "We have to go inside. We just have to squeeze through this small gap." He pointed into the cave.

Hunter took off his bag and handed it to Taz. He pushed himself through the narrow gap and then signaled Taz to follow. Taz called to Moja to come as well. She lifted her head from the ground she was sniffing and then crawled through the gap with ease. Inside the cavern, the three explorers looked at the stone walls for any clues. Then Hunter saw it; a blue glow highlighted an area in the far corner. He stood in a trance-like state for a few seconds. Taz couldn't see the blue glow. To him, it just looked like a normal rock.

"This is the answer to my dreams," Hunter said slowly. The strange way in which he spoke, caught Taz's attention.

"What did you say?" Taz looked at Hunter.

"Follow me, it's through here." Hunter walked over to the area in the corner and reached out with his left hand. The blue glow extended around his arm and then the solid rock faded. It revealed an entrance to a deep underground tunnel.

"What the hell?" Taz was very confused at what he had just witnessed. "I see a tunnel, but also the rock. It's like a hologram or something?" Hunter stepped inside and looked back at Taz. He laughed slightly in disbelief. "How did you do that?" Taz asked.

"It's fine, you can just step through, bring Moja. We're going to need the torches from your bag. It's dark down here." Taz reached in his bag and activated the torches. He put a rope around Moja's neck and guided her to the entrance. They could see Hunter on the other side, slightly distorted through the rocks illusion. Taz timidly stepped through and was surprised that Moja jumped through the rock without hesitation. On the other side, Taz handed Hunter a torch, and they walked down the long dark tunnel.

The air was moist and the stone walls were cool and damp. The walls were not natural. They had been hand carved many years ago. As they made their way deeper into the crevasse, they reached the end of the tunnel. There was an entrance to a large open area deep underground.

"Look at those symbols." Taz pointed to some strange markings carved into the rock above their heads. "They're similar to the symbols on the metal disc my Uncle gave you. How is that possible?" Hunter gazed at them for a moment.

"I've been here before…" He said to Taz and partly to himself.

"You can remember?" Taz couldn't believe it.

"No, but I can feel it. I know this place. Everything I've been looking for is in here." Hunter looked at the symbols, while Taz pulled out a small notepad from his pocket, and began writing them down.

They entered the open are which was more like a gigantic temple. The space was humongous and the ceiling was higher than they could see. The walls were metallic and had intricate artistic patterns. Some parts looked futuristic, industrial, and not of this world. Small sections of the wall sparkled with a blue glow and illuminated the area. Hunter and Taz didn't need their torches anymore. A raised path led to a large platform with a dark entrance on the other side. Either side was a long drop, down to deep still water, which sparkled in the blue light. They walked along the path with Hunter leading the way. It was wide and stable, but Taz was still nervous about falling in. Moja walked calmly behind them.

When they reached the platform, they looked at the large space surrounding them. Around the edge of the platform were several large jewels evenly spaced. The patterns on the walls seemed to take a more recognizable form. It looked like a giant painting, like something the artist might have painted in his cabin. In the center of the picture was a large crystal on a pedestal. On the left side was a knight wielding a large sword, kneeling at the foot of the crystal. On the right, it looked like a moon floating in space, surrounded by stars which glistened majestically in the phthalo blue light.

"Stay here, I must enter alone." Hunter spoke to Taz while looking at the entrance on the other side of the platform, which appeared to lead to a dead end. Taz said nothing, as he watched Hunter step inside. There was a soft hum, followed by a flash blue light, then Hunter vanished.

"Hunter!" Taz screamed. He looked into the entrance, which was now empty, and cautiously moved closer. He took off his backpack and tried to get as close as he could without stepping inside. Taz could see the floor was metallic. He picked up a small rock and threw it into the entrance. Nothing happened. Moja stood patiently acting strangely calm. Then she lay down on the platform in a total state of relaxation and closed her eyes.

As Taz debated in his mind whether he should step inside,

there was another flash of blue light. Smoke filled the opening and Taz trembled in fear as he imagined what might appear from behind the fog. Then Hunter staggered out and fell into his arms.

"Are you ok Hunter!? What was that?" Taz couldn't be sure if what he had seen had actually taken place. Hunter put his hand on his head and tried to speak.

"...I've just met..." He mumbled and then regained some form of consciousness. "Taz...I think I have what I came for...I might need some help, but we can leave now." Hunter put his arm around Taz and then slowly walked back along the path. His head was throbbing and his mind was confused and disorientated.

"Hold on, one second, I need to get my bag." Taz carefully left Hunter, while he went back to the platform to retrieve his backpack. He looked in every direction and checked that Hunter wasn't watching him. Then he quickly picked up one of the large jewels from the edge and placed it in his bag.

When they reached the tunnel, which led back up to the surface, Hunter needed to take a rest and leaned against the wall.

"What happened to you? It looked like you disappeared." Taz offered him some water.

"It felt like an eternity," Hunter looked at his hands. "I'm not sure if it was just a vision or if it really happened. I met someone inside. He was waiting for me."

"Who was it?" Taz asked.

"I don't know who he was, but he seemed familiar. He told me his name was...Toki. He said he had a gift for me. Then it was like a thousand images entered my mind. It looked like the most beautiful, peaceful place you could imagine. But then it changed. It started to burn and fade away. This person, Toki, was dueling with someone on a stairway that went into the sky. Then everything vanished and it was just me and Toki. He handed me a crystal shard and faded away."

"That sounds intense. Do you want to rest here for the night?"

"No, I can make it. Help me up. My head is starting to feel better." Taz helped Hunter to his feet, who then clicked his fingers back at him. It was a signal they both understood. A way for Hunter to tell Taz he was going to be fine.

They walked slowly up through the tunnel until they reached the entrance back at the surface. It had started to rain with thunder and lightning. The wind was blowing much harder and the sun had completely set. Shortly before they reached the top, Moja pulled hard on the rope Taz was using as a leash and broke free from his grip. She ran ahead out through the rocks, while Taz cried out in vain for her to come back. As Hunter and Taz quickened their pace, they could hear her growling and barking amongst the sounds of the wind and rain.

When they exited back out into the open, they saw Moja taking a defensive stance. They were then shocked to see a dark figure standing under the old tree.

"I sensed you were here." The figure spoke with a deep, yet somewhat, withered voice. He was wearing a black cloak surrounded by a red shroud of mist. The figure was completely motionless until he reached up with his hands. The shroud faded and he revealed himself to Hunter and Taz. He looked old and pale. His face was partially covered by the hood of his cloak. His eyes were transparent and he stared directly at Hunter.

"Taz get behind me!" Hunter tried to strengthen his body.

"Now you are ready." The figure looked down at Moja, as she growled at him.

"What are you talking about? Who are you? What are you doing here?" Hunter yelled, with a weakened voice.

"You still don't remember?" The man let out a brief and controlled laugh.

"...Are you my enemy?" Hunter was confused and did not trust him.

"Don't worry human, I'm not here to hurt you. I'm here to fulfil a promise I made a long time ago and help you on your journey."

"How can you help me?"

"You must travel to a place called Tech City. It's far east from here. There you will find the answers."

"Do you know who I am? Do you know where I come from?"

"You wouldn't understand even if I told you. I have kept my promise, but I cannot stay here any longer, he is watching. Now I must return to my sanctuary and pay for my sins until the end of my days." As the dark figure walked away, he paused and looked down towards the ground. "I am sorry for what I have done." Then he faded into the dark night sky. Hunter, Taz, and Moja stood, as lightning struck the ground around them and the rain fell heavy.

~

"After the strange man left, we traveled back to Valley

Village. We spent a few days there and I managed to convince my Uncle to let me go with Hunter to Tech City. We took a boat from Lyme Cove and traveled along the coast to get here. We sold the jewel I took to a local jeweler, who paid a ridiculously high price for it."

"Was that Dante?" Nakita asked.

"Yeah, do you know him?"

"Not really, it doesn't matter. Taz, your story is very interesting. Who was the man in the black cloak?" Nakita had finished her glass of milk.

"We don't know. We never saw him again." He shrugged his shoulders.

"So that's why you originally came to Tech City. Do you think he knew about Alex and Project Overlord?"

"Possibly, but I think he may have also meant for us to meet you." Taz placed the book from Nakita's father on the table.

"Me? What could I possibly have to do with all this?"

"It's all in this book. It's full of symbols like the ones we saw inside the temple. I was able to use this to translate what they say. It doesn't make much sense now, but I think if I study it for longer, it might help us in some way."

"That is a very strange coincidence." Nakita held the book in her hands.

"Hunter doesn't think this is related to our mission in Capitol City, but it's too big of a coincidence to ignore." Taz said.

"It's strange, I didn't keep anything from my father except

for this book…Taz, I'm pretty tired. I think I'm going to go to sleep. Does Moja sleep in your room?"

"Yeah, I'll take her. I'm pretty tired too. I'll see you tomorrow Nakita."

"Goodnight Taz, thank you for telling me your story."

Upstairs, Hunter lay in his bed. His body had almost recovered and was in a deep sleep. Although his body was resting peacefully, his mind was highly active. He was having a vivid dream. A woman who resembled Nakita was kneeling by a river. She was washing her clothes and noticed Hunter staring at her. She smiled at him and then everything around her went pitch black. The smile left her face and was replaced by fear. She looked directly at Hunter, as her face began to mutate into a grotesque monster. She laughed hysterically at him, while her eyes burned with Alizarin Crimson. When she spoke, it was not her voice, but the voice of someone else. She ridiculed and taunted him.

"You'll never beat me. I've already won."

Hunter woke up at the sound of his door opening.

"Taz, is that you?" The room was dark. When he sat up, he could see the silhouette was much too tall to be Taz. It was Nakita. She walked slowly into his room and closed the door behind her.

"Nakita? Is everything ok?" She slid her small black jacket down her arms and placed it on a chair. Her white tank top and black miniskirt hugged the contours of her body. She knew exactly how to stand to make men want her.

"I'm fine, I'm just feeling a little strange. Can I talk to you?" She stood at the foot of his bed and looked into his eyes. He slowly stood up and pointed to an armchair in the corner of his room.

"Why don't you sit down. I'll turn the lights on." She sat in the chair and leaned forward towards him while he sat on the edge of his bed.

"You know, when I said that I had no idea about Alex and Project Overlord, I was lying. I knew he was up to something. There were so many clues, but I chose to ignore them. I didn't care. All I thought about, was that I needed to stay with him because he was rich and powerful. I ignored so many bad things he did. At some point, I lost myself in all of it. I don't know who I am anymore. I need to make things right. At first, I thought I wanted to come with you to Capitol City so I could help rescue the children. But that was also a lie. I'm not going for them. I'm going for me. I want to go so I can redeem myself. So I can prove to myself that I can do good things and change my life. It all probably sounds very egotistical." She couldn't look at Hunter while she spoke.

"At least you're being honest. I can't say that my reasons for doing all this are completely selfless either. I'm also partly doing this for myself. To try and find out who I am and where I come from. We may have our own vested interest in this, but if we also help to save those children, then I think there's nothing wrong with that."

Nakita looked at Hunter with a smile and nodded her head. She felt genuinely positive about what Hunter had just said. He paused for a moment and then decided the time was right.

"Nakita, I need to tell you something. You can't come with me to Capitol City." She stopped smiling. "This is going to be very dangerous. I need you to take Taz back to Valley Village. He won't listen to me if I tell him to go. That's why I'm leaving tonight by myself. In the morning, I need you to explain to him that I'm sorry, but that I'll be back as soon as it's over. He can't come after me. On top of that skyscraper I realized that I was incredibly foolish. If these people are targeting children, that puts Taz in incredible danger. They're very smart for targeting war orphans because no one would notice if they disappeared. It would be the same for Taz and I can't let that happen. Nakita, when I first saw you, I thought you were the most beautiful woman I'd ever seen. I need you to help me. You can do something good without actually having to fight. Just make sure Taz gets home safely. I'll take care of the rest."

Nakita understood what he was saying. She felt sad, but deep down, she knew he was right.

"...what about Moja?" She asked softly.

"Make sure Taz takes good care of her. She's a special dog. I'll miss her. Taz really loves her, but he won't admit it." Hunter laughed slightly and stood up. "You can take a boat from here all the way to Lyme Cove. Valley Village isn't far from there. After that, you're free to do whatever you want. Goodbye Nakita, I hope I'll see you again."

She stood up, walked towards him, and reached out to hold his hands. She leaned in and kissed him on the lips.

"Goodbye Hunter, until we meet again."

Hunter reached into his bag and pulled out an envelope.

"Give this to Taz. He'll know what it means."

Hunter left his room and quietly walked down the stairs past Taz's room. Inside, Taz was fast asleep and snoring loudly. Moja woke up and lifted her head, while her ears pointed straight up. She felt something was not right.

Hunter left the tavern and walked through the streets of

Berlin alone in the pale moonlight. The air had a slight mist and he faded out of sight into the black, ready to embark on the next chapter of his journey.

CAPITOL CITY

The planet of Eros is made up of three huge continents. To the south is a desolate wasteland considered the most dangerous place on the planet. In the middle is a continent divided into two halves. The western side is a mixture of towns and cities scattered amongst great wildlife, mountains, and rivers. The dominant city in this part of the world is Kunsthof. The eastern side of Middle Continent is a vast desert where the great city of Tiberia once stood. Tech City lies in the center between the two halves of Middle Continent. To the north is a continent filled almost completely by a single city.

The city is so large that it is divided into many sub-divisions called districts. They are like cities within the city. It is far greater in size and population than Tech City. On the outskirts are slums that extend for hundreds of miles. As you approach the center the buildings grow taller and the streets become more densely populated. It's a place where corporations are the most powerful entities in society. Corruption rules this place. It's a place where dreams are made and hopes can be shattered in an instant. The name of the place is Capitol City.

Deep in the capitol is a large corporate facility, which is part of the governments military. General Ryuu is sitting at his desk inside a large executive office on the top floor. He stands up and looks out of the floor to ceiling windows at the city below him. From here, he can see far and wide across Capitol City. Ryuu is a tall man with short dark hair and a large scar on the right side of his face. His eyes are full of darkness.

"Sir, we have some important news." A high-ranking official enters the office. Ryuu turns from the window to face him. He's silent but nods his head. "General Ryuu, we've lost contact with our operatives in Tech City. They've all been killed." Ryuu turns back to look at the city again and speaks with a deep slow voice.

"That's not a problem. We have enough samples for the project. What's the latest from Professor Arturo?"

"Everything is proceeding according to plan, sir."

"And what about the specimen?" The General narrows his eyes.

"Arturo reports it is reacting within normal parameters, sir."

"Good, tell the board we will begin as soon as possible." Ryuu signals the officer to leave the room.

"Of course, thank you General." The officer leaves, closing the door behind him. General Ryuu stands staring out of the window. He is not looking at the city beneath him, but rather at his own reflection. In his eyes he sees the image of a burning fortress in the sky. It consumes him.

"Where are you?"

ABOUT THE AUTHOR

Will Wallner is a musician, entrepreneur, and author. He grew up in South West England and spent many years living in Los Angeles as a rock musician. Now he resides in Berlin, Germany where he manages several companies throughout Europe.

He loves nothing more than to spend time with his animals, and to plug a Les Paul into a loud Marshall amplifier. Whether he's recording new music, starting a new business, or writing a new book, he is always in the process of creating something new. That is what inspires him. For more information visit www.willwallner.com

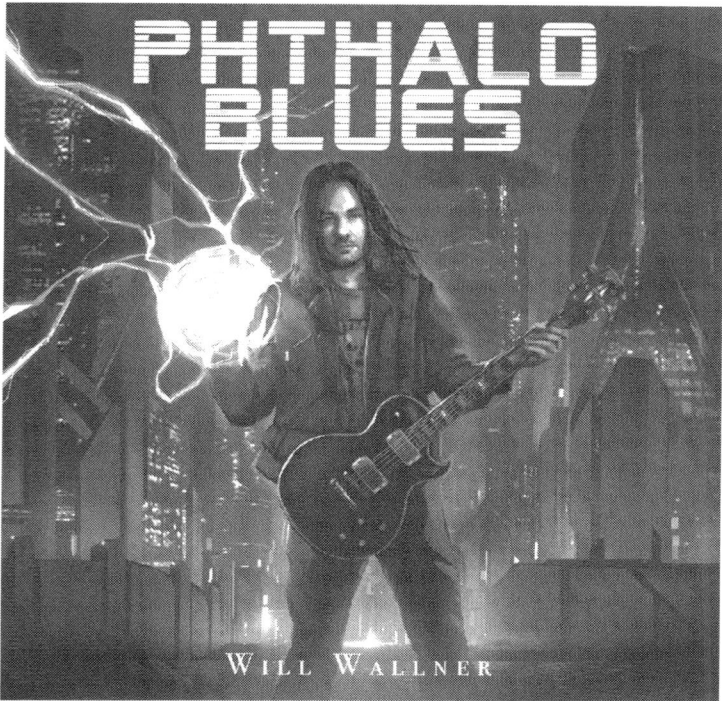

COMIC SERIES - COMING SOON

WILD FRONTIER

A series of brutal murders are terrorizing the citizens of Capitol City. Detective Sykes is sent to investigate and uncovers a deadly conspiracy within his own police department.

Wild Frontier tells the story of Detective Sykes who has recently been promoted and hand-picked by the President to catch a serial killer, who is terrorizing the citizens of Capitol City. As he delves deeper into the case, Sykes uncovers a sinister plot within his own police department to conceal evidence related to the murders. As Sykes visits each new crime scene, he learns more about the killer and the conspiracy against him. Sykes doesn't know who he can trust but one thing is clear, this killer is unlike anything he's ever seen before and must be stopped.

For more information visit www.phthalo-blues.com

Made in the USA
Columbia, SC
20 April 2018